THE DA|

MALCOLM HOLLINGDRAKE

Thank you.

Book Twelve in the Harrogate Crime Series

i

ISBN 978-1-3999-2924-0

Also by Malcolm Hollingdrake

Bridging the Gulf

Shadows from the Past

Short Stories for Short Journeys

The Harrogate Crime Series

Only the Dead

Hell's Gate

Flesh Evidence

Game Point

Dying Art

Crossed Out

The Third Breath

Treble Clef

Threadbare

Fragments

Uncertainty of Reason

The Merseyside Series – Published by Hobeck Books

Catch as Catch Can

Syn

Dedicated to

John Marshall Barlow and Jacqueline Ann Barlow.

Thank you for your continued support.

Tears are often the telescope by which men see far
into heaven.

Henry Ward Beecher

This also might be said for them seeing far into the
depths of hell!

DCI Cyril Bennett

Never let the doubters win!

Prologue

My dear teacher,

Today was the best and the worst day of my life! I'm sure you remember very well the three o'clock boy perched aloft but far from aloof. You looked up as I down. I was the boy, alone and rejected, rejected, that is, apart from you and some of your caring colleagues.

Where has the time gone? Only now, when my world seems more in focus, do I remember how much they all fought for me, a fight against the odds – ignoring my anger and impossible ways you could see through the shadows. I just wanted to tell you, sir, I was listening!

How we change as we grow!

I'm sorry and hope you can forgive me

Chapter 1

The walk home to Robert Street from the police station, set on the outskirts of Harrogate, seemed on this particular day, endless. DCI Cyril Bennett quickened his pace whilst watching the remnants of the day slip away; fortunately, the light was fading more quickly than his energy. Myriad dying colours had contrived to force the evening sky to surrender to the dark. The traffic grew heavier, the cars, like small creatures, scampered on their way, their lights adding to the night-time's rich palette.

Cyril crossed The Stray, the arrow-straight footpath led from the corner of Otley Road to West Park, one of the many that traversed the vast expanse of urban green. He paused at the point where two paths intersected; a solitary street lamp smeared a butter-coloured light around itself, an island of warmth, before it faded across the neighbouring litter bin bringing to it an elongated, deformed shadow. He glanced around before looking towards the heaven's pitchy blackness. Even in the lamplight, the many stars appeared to puncture the now expansive shroud-black canopy.

A frown crossed his brow as he searched, scanning sections of night sky until identifying the Great Bear – Ursa

Major – "The Plough," he said with a satisfying smile. He had known it his whole life; it was the first constellation his mother had picked from the heavens when they stood together in the garden. As a young child, they would stand and she would sing to him – 'Twinkle, twinkle, little star ...' The words danced in his head as he remembered his mother's delicate, musician's finger pause at each star as she sang. The seven syllables matching the seven stars. "Septentrio," he said out loud, his mother's words drifting into his consciousness. The Romans had called it the *seven plough oxen,* and Cyril knew it as The Plough. His eyes followed two of the seven stars until he focused on Polaris, the pole star.

"Time to be guided home, Bennett. It's been a long day." Leaving the warmth and solitude The Stray offered, he headed towards the many lights that lined the main road leading through the centre of Harrogate. In ten minutes, he would be home. Holding his watch to catch the last of the lamplight he checked the time, shook his wrist before checking again. He was still not used to this latest addition on his wrist, in some ways he missed the old Explorer Two. It would take time to acclimatise to the new watch, he knew that.

The passageway between the buildings was always a conduit for a cool breeze, it was a micro climate in both temperature and darkness. A streetlight thief crept its way into the passage encouraging Cyril to give necessary chase whilst quickening his pace before emerging onto Robert Street. It was good to be home. He felt the tension begin to evaporate the closer he got.

The light in the hall was on and Julie's car was in its

usual place. He glanced briefly skywards but clouds had concealed the stars.

"You're late, Cyril. Everything okay?" Julie's voice drifted along the passageway escorted as if by a subtle cooking aroma.

"Missing person. Two days, Julie, and they've only just let us know she's AWOL. I can never understand why they leave it so long. It's not as if they've popped to the shops! Young girl too, nineteen. They believed she was staying at her boyfriend's house according to a text message they'd received. A text? Why don't young folk speak?"

"That's what kids do these days, besides, how old did you say, nineteen?"

He crossed the kitchen, slipped his arms around her and kissed her neck. "N-n-n-n-n nineteen as the song said."

"Cupboard love as per usual. Song? Just how old are you, Bennett?"

"When I was a young kid, I loved it. You weren't born then. 'The average age of the American soldier fighting in Vietnam was ...'" He did not finish.

"She's an adult. Your favourite wine tonight too. In the fridge. I do spoil you."

Cyril immediately checked his mental calendar for important dates. He could think of none.

"Am I missing something?" He held the bottle, the condensation frosting the green glass and a low whistle came to his lips. "Schoenheitz. Gewürtzraminer. My favourite."

"Ordered half a case. Today, Cyril, we remember the visit I made to Wihr-au-Val. It was after Liz's death. Out of such sadness grew what we have today." She turned and her eyes spoke volumes. "It was the moment when I knew for certain I loved you, DCI Bennett. Today is the anniversary of the day I arrived to find you. I watched as you walked away from the train, a man lost and broken. A sword of guilt hovered above you. I wept for you."

Cyril stared at the amber coloured label whilst running his finger along the elegant shape of the bottle, neither seeing nor feeling in the moment. His emotions collided. The thoughts of his mother earlier and now the memory of Liz. It was as if the stars had aligned to bring a tear to his eye.

Julie saw and heeded the situation. "This is just another step, my hero, in the healing process." She knew he needed neither sympathy nor melancholy but he did require support to take the next steps to break free of the moment. She slid the corkscrew across the table. "Before it gets warm. We need to drink, not look." Her voice neither questioned nor condoned but it was the push he needed.

Chapter 2

2006

The endless sky directly above gave no focal point by which to define distance; neither vapour trails nor clouds were present, just a reassuring vacuum of calming blue. A dizzying hue grew in strength the further towards the vertical he stared.

Eyes scanned inquisitively. His head dropped slowly towards the horizontal, the silent level where the ethereal met a hazy reality. It seemed non-threatening, distant and diluted as if smudged with a graphite covered finger. As his gaze moved closer to his everyday surroundings, they grew sharper, more focused and so too his anger returned, its claws tearing his stomach bringing the nausea to his throat and with the closing proximity came claustrophobia and fear.

He wrapped his legs within his arms as he perched on the roof's ridge, his back reassuringly lodged against the brick chimney; silhouetted and bird-like. Eyes watched and he knew they did, not out of curiosity, but concern. He neither cared nor returned their stare. At this moment, they were nothing, nobody, insignificant at this critical time of the day and they were powerless to help, unable to intervene when his needs were at their greatest.

Up here where the breeze caressed with a welcome gentleness was a freedom. "If only I could spread wings and push against the slippery slates and soar." The words were whispered but intense. For the briefest of moments, the anguish seemed to be exorcised by the uncertainty of the possibilities that were way beyond this horizon and that of his childish dreams. Reality, as always, was his true friend yet in so many ways his frustrating enemy, an enemy that held him back from living a life he knew he feared to live. He remained firmly perched.

Taking the thin cardboard tube, removed earlier from the craft box, he put it to his eye and closed the other. The world was now reduced, more manageable. Scanning the car park, he concentrated on the first taxi as it entered the gate. It crawled round the other parked vehicles; like a predator preparing to eat it would soon take up its normal position. Then came another and another. Like sand through an hourglass they arrived emphasising the passing of another disappointing day and forewarning of the possible nightmare that was to come. He turned slowly and the viewed objects moved with an unnatural speed until he stopped at the face that had stared up at him since his arrival. It was familiar and non-threatening but anxiety returned to the pit of his stomach. He usually watched but if not him then another teacher – normally whoever was on duty – like a guardian and as regular as the taxis.

Placing a finger over the open end of the tube brought immediate darkness and with it a security, a confirmed darkness bringing the ending he could control – light, dark, light, dark – all with one, small movement. Removing the tube from his eye he stuffed it down his shirt. It would now be his imaginary friend, his kindred Kaleidoscope, magic and colourful, to take him away from this life.

The cars came as they always did. His anger grew as more taxis appeared. He rocked back and forth, his backside planted firmly on the ridge tiles, his feet on the opposing sloping slates. Sticking his thumb into his mouth he allowed his finger to rub the already damaged bridge of his nose until he felt the burn. To Christian this action exaggerated his silhouetted face against the blue of the sky, his hand becoming beak-like changing the boy into a roosting bird.

The rubbing, slow at first, grew faster and with greater force as he rocked in time to the action of his finger. The nasal scab never had time to heal; it would never have time. Blood trickled from the end of his nose before being caught on his tongue. The metallic, copper taste brought with it a reassurance. He had tasted this tang for as long as he could remember. No one seemed to care, no one really knew. They would never stop it happening even when they said they would. One day, however, he vowed that he would.

Some of the children leaving school looked up and pointed, but not many. They knew he was there; they were told to ignore him with a teacher's smile to reward their obedience, a house point for listening and responding to instruction.

"Ignore him, he's just a silly boy seeking attention!"

One by one the taxis departed each now with the same children they had deposited at the inner gate of Willow Fold School just six hours previously. Soon there would be only the teachers, the caretaker and him – the boy on the roof. His taxi waited. The driver leaned against the car whilst he talked with the Deputy Headteacher. Eyes occasionally looked up and heads shook. It would end the way it always did. He would win, the taxi would depart. Going home, if that was what it was – home, would be delayed just a little longer.

The teachers knew it was a cry for help but there was little that could be done. Social Services compounded that.

Chapter 3

2006

Fiona sat waiting for the remaining professionals to take their seats around the table. The meeting was due to start at two. She looked at the name on the file and the accompanying photograph and remembered the first day the boy had arrived at the school. She had been summoned to the school hall. Gym bars lined one wall, row upon row of horizontal wooden bars next to a number of tied back ropes and ladders. The welfare staff readied the room for lunch and ignored the boy. Tables now filled the space and the aroma of the meal, cooked on site, filled the air. Sandra, the school cook, had been there a long time and few things surprised her. She leaned on the hatch watching the child cling to the upper bar.

"It's beans, beans, I can smell 'em, beans, beans." He thrust his backside away from the bars. "Beans make you fart." He then continued to make the appropriate rasping noise as loudly as possible. Fiona had watched him for a while before chatting to Sandra as if oblivious to the boy above her and close to the ceiling. His inability to shock, shocked him. This behaviour in his mainstream school would have brought the Head and other staff – he would be the centre of attention and outrage but here in the special school setting things were different.

"Let me know if he comes down in five minutes, Sandra. If he does, he can eat, if not his beans will go to the other well-behaved children." Fiona raised her voice for all in the hall to hear. She left the hall and the boy clinging to the bars watched her until she closed the far door. Seeing he was now being ignored he climbed down, retreated to a corner before pulling his sweater over his head. He rocked slowly.

After ten minutes Fiona returned. She crouched before him.

"Thank you for listening." She touched the child's knee. "Hungry?"

The sweater moved back and forth.

"Let's get those hands washed."

"Sorry, miss." He pulled the sweater down and turned to Sandra. "Sorry."

He received a smile.

***

The last person took their seat and the meeting started.

"The boy shows all the symptoms of domestic cruelty." Fiona Grimes tapped the file positioned on the desk. "You've seen the school diary of events. He needs psychological support. We've witnessed unusual behaviour during play therapy sessions, not only on a one-to-one basis but when with others, with both adults and when with his peers.

"I'd like to draw your attention to emphasise the family dynamic. We have one young boy in a family of four adult females, his mother and three siblings. He has a mother who according to the father, may well be soliciting not only herself but her three girls, the youngest of whom is eighteen. However, we only have his suggestion of that and no real evidence."

Fiona was determined to highlight every element affecting the boy. Those on the panel listened. They were a collection of professionals brought together to discuss and plan the child's future.

"The home seems stable enough whenever I visit," the social worker mumbled as she fiddled with a pen. "Granted, I never see a male present but Jamie visits his father for a day a week. I've witnessed him in both settings. Both homes are clean, warm and both parents appear to love the child."

Fiona stiffened. No matter what evidence she presented this particular social worker seemed to block any further investigation. "What differences does he exhibit when in the different households?" She failed to calm her growing frustration.

"Mother says he likes being alone in his room. He's a normal little boy."

"A 'normal little boy'." She made the inverted comma signs with her fingers. "A boy who attends a special school for children with emotional and behavioural issues is classified as normal. In your professional capacity in what ways do you subscribe to that?" The words came short and sharp.

The social worker raised an eyebrow. "He's quiet, she knows that and is not naïve enough to believe the unsavoury breakdown of her marriage was probably the catalyst for his behavioural troubles in school. She's aware that she is partially responsible and wants to help, she wants to allow him time."

"Time? What time is this of which she speaks? The same time that is supposedly the universal healer of all things?" Fiona failed to withdraw the cynicism in her voice as the sentences were uttered. They were like shots fired at point blank range in quick succession. "You've read the school reports? What about the men who come and go? That's when he's to remain in his room. We know why too. You've seen the disfigurement of his nose." Fiona turned to the doctor.

"Direct result of stress and insecurity: thumb sucking and rubbing the bridge of his nose until raw for a child of his age, it's a common trait – insecurity. It's in the file. From the medical reports there's no evidence of sexual activity but we feel sure from the evidence, he has and probably still does witness inappropriate adult interaction. Now whether that is visual or audible we cannot say but the findings from the play therapy sessions supports his having an inappropriate understanding of sex for his age. I'm also aware it could be argued that many children who have unsupervised use of a computer can witness these things but professionally, I sense there is something more fundamental in his actions."

Eyes turned to Linda Morrison, the school play therapist, before Fiona interjected.

"Maybe he still witnesses inappropriate adult interaction." Fiona had let the words tumble in her head briefly. "That's like saying 'almost certainly', it's either he has or he might have. You feel sure he might!" She threw her pen onto the file and faced Linda.

Linda raised a hand. "You'll all have read my extended

report detailing some of the behaviours exhibited during unstructured, unsupervised yet monitored play sessions. Although he avoided certain items within the play area, he did take the anatomical dolls from the shelf. We witnessed inappropriate play with the dolls and I know you'll say that research will suggest we cannot make judgements from those actions as many children, both sexes, will do that when alone. Boys will make a willy if you give them a ball of clay but they soon move on after a few giggles.

"My concern is the length of time this activity has continued. We also have modelled play periods after Jamie has spent greater time with his father – extended holiday visiting – and you will see a marked difference in his play and his general attitude towards certain elements of that play. If you look at page nineteen, you can read of six contrasting sessions, three after spending extended time with his father. To put them into context the sessions were viewed through the two-way mirror. They were planned, solitary open-ended play sessions. There was, you'll note, a need to keep them solitary as we found he would withdraw when other children either known to him or unknown are introduced. So, after extended paternal visits there appears a more regular attitude to his play. He focuses more on the cars and the road map. He seems calmer and there were fewer occasions where he sucked his thumb. Now in contrast, the sessions directly after these when he returns to be with his mother, Jamie brings to the room a collection of cardboard tubes. If you read on, you'll see my concerns."

The meeting went on longer than anticipated and there seemed little consensus. Fiona collected the papers and slipped them into her briefcase. She hung her head as the frustration bled from every part of her being. The agencies seemed to be listening but none were hearing. They seldom challenged the parents no matter how plainly the child signalled. Being the SENCO could be the best job in the world but on days like these she wondered why she bothered. She needed to discuss the outcome with the Head if she were back in school. Fiona tapped on the Headteacher's door. There was no answer.

"She's out."

Fiona gasped, momentarily startled by the Deputy Head who had appeared in the corridor. "You're as silent as smoke!"

"Sorry! She's out. Another meeting so it must be another working school day and considering the time of that working day, I somehow doubt she will tackle the traffic to come back here. If we're in luck, she will deign to inform us of her movements." Christian never let his face slip. "Your trouble, Fiona, if I may be so bold, is that you see good in everyone. Now I'm not saying that's a bad thing as kids like these need good people like you and you're a bloody good SENCO. What they don't need is Dorothy the almighty. Anyway, I've been called as there's the usual problem. Our boy has left the classroom and I can only presume he's heading for the roof. As I sit to the right hand of Dorothy the almighty, I'll be happy to help and discuss your panel meeting when I've sorted out the problem." He checked his watch. "It's escape to the roof time and that Fiona has to take priority!"

"Thanks. Your name suits your position but honestly, Christian, you're appreciated and you keep this place afloat so never forget it. If only we had more like you to fight the cause."

"I'm flattered but I know I have the emotional scars, Fiona. I'll expect my reward in heaven, I guess, as I sure as hell won't get it here."

"You'll have to get there first and from what you say, our boyo is closer to God than you at this minute. I'll drop the file onto your desk, discuss it tomorrow for what that will be worth. I must also dash once the kids are in the taxis."

The words fell on deaf ears as Christian pushed through the door leading him into the playground. The boy, high on the roof's ridge, stared down. It was going to be another extended day.

Chapter 4

DI David Owen sat at his desk and looked at the framed photograph of the baby. It was alongside an ultrasound image in a black twin frame. It was hard to comprehend that they were of one and the same. Pride seemed to ooze from his pores as he lifted the frame to take a closer look, something he now did on a regular basis. It did not go unnoticed by his team. It reminded him of a photograph his Nan had on her sideboard beneath a glass cabinet of crockery that was to be used only for best. He pulled a face mimicking that of the child. Shakti watched from across the open-plan office. She felt too voyeuristic for comfort but neither could she resist. The approach of Cyril Bennett made her duck back behind the screen.

It had been two months since The Sprog, Owen's term of endearment, was born and he could not wait to get home after his shift just to look at him. Was it normal that he wanted to cry with sheer joy every time he thought of the boy?

Pausing, Cyril watched his colleague replace the frame and adjust its position before receiving a welcome look, a smile and a cheery greeting. "Growing by the day, sir. Who'd have thought that that could become …?" He flipped the frame round. "Never thought about the wonders of nature until now. Bloody marvellous really."

"Small things make grown men turn from the darkness to the light!" Cyril mumbled just loud enough for Owen to hear.

It brought only a frown. Owen grabbed his jar of sweets and offered one to Cyril. "Mint?"

"And some fell on stony ground, Owen, but yes, a mint is much needed. Remind me to ask April to have a word with you about the road to Damascus." Unwrapping the sweet, he dropped the wrapper back into the mug. "Tea in five and bring with you any intel you have on the missing girl."

Owen looked in the mug and retrieved the empty wrapper. He stood and looked across at Shakti. "Came through here like it were a public convenience!" he grumbled, ensuring those near could hear before screwing up the small wrapper and aiming it with no accuracy at the waste bin. He winked before disappearing towards the kitchen.

Within the specified time, Owen moved cautiously through the door of Cyril's office, a crockery rattle proceeding his progress. The saucer was awash with tea. Putting his mug on the mat he poured the slops back into the cup and popped the cup and saucer in front of Cyril who placed his head in one hand as if summoning spiritual help.

"Thank you. I wonder if our Queen receives the same service with her morning Darjeeling? And the missing girl?"

Owen collected a chair and placed a file on the desk. "Sadie Vance. Missing since –" he flicked open the file whilst sipping his tea – "didn't arrive home Tuesday but according to her mother she would often stay with her boyfriend. She received a text message to that effect. Has a twin sister, Blanche." He paused before repeating the name, "Blanche Vance. Seems a bit old fashioned for one so young."

Cyril did not need to speak. He had thought that about his own name since childhood but controlled the conversation with his facial expression. It was as if they had worked together too long and Owen picked up all of the cues and every nuance and responded accordingly, not dissimilar to a theatrical double act, one straight, the other the comedian.

"Nineteen. Works in a cafe on Cambridge Road. Boyfriend is John Thompson … lives …" he flicked through the file again. "Lives just off Whinney Lane." He read the address. "Relatively new property. These estates are springing up everywhere. Soon Harrogate will be a part of Leeds if they carry on building at the rate they are! Some, to my inexperienced eye, even look to be made of wood and brown paper and then clad in bricks!" He drained the remnants of his mug.

"Search advisor? Search strategy developed?"

Owen tapped the file. "Carruthers, sir. As it has to be a DI leading that will be me. All the checks have been done and family liaison is in place and after forty-eight hours we'll have round the clock point of call for those concerned."

"Let's hope it doesn't go that far," Cyril grumbled. "Have you posted details on the police website and social media giving a full description and stressing we are treating it as a high-risk missing person? Thompson and his parents have been questioned, cafe personnel too? Press releases?" He barely paused for breath before he flicked open the file.

"In the process of, sir."

Owen's mobile rang. As he listened, he mouthed the name, *Smirthwaite,* to Cyril. "Get them to run ANPR checks for the scooter. Then get an image of the bike or similar bike and add it to the missing person page and the general sites and keep them updated."

"Apparently, she travels to and from the cafe on a scooter, white. According to Brian's interview, she has a Vespa, she got it whilst she's learning to drive. He's posting a full description and Traffic is aware. If she's using it, then it shouldn't take long to track down. Her parents tried to persuade her not to have it but she usually gets what she wants. She told them that at her age she needed her independence when they offered to taxi her."

"Coming back from work?"

Owen nodded. "According to her parents."

"Regular time, Owen?"

"Just after five thirty. Always that time apart from Wednesday when she works a half day. Doesn't work Sunday."

"Do we know if she takes the same route? Check the number against ANPR for the last ..." he paused. "How long has she had the scooter?"

Owen flicked through the file. "Five weeks."

"That's how far we go back, five weeks. Mobile number for the girl?" Cyril sipped more tea before steepling his fingers. They were restless since giving up vaping. The craving for nicotine was still strong but it was the need to have something in his hands that brought the greatest frustration.

"Nothing, it's switched off. The boyfriend tried to track it as you do through the app but nothing. Waiting to receive phone records as soon as. Her laptop has been brought from home and hopefully we'll soon track her search and email history. Looking into her social media activity too."

"Friends other than the lad, Thompson?"

"Parents gave a list. It's here." He tapped the file. "We're contacting each one but hopefully the call to the public should shed some light." He emphasised the word 'light'.

Cyril moved his cup and saucer towards Owen, a signal. "Do we know her last position by the final use of the phone?"

"We await."

"I want Thompson's phone records too and his stored photograph records looked at – cloud storage too. I'm sure he'll co-operate. I take it we've searched both her and the lad's addresses?

"Sir, nothing." He raised his eyebrows as if she would be likely to be hiding in either place. "Mother says she only took what she stood in."

"Thanks, Owen. Do you think it's a cry for help?" His eyes did not convey the same meaning as his words. He had been a copper for too long to take things for granted. "Many people go missing for just that."

Owen took the hint. "But we can't take that risk." He pushed the file in the opposite direction.

"And Owen, check DVLA to see who owned the scooter before her. Have you checked her place of work – she did go?"

Owen let his head nod. "Sir, will check."

***

The heavy smell of fried bacon lingered heavily in the air,

gone was the appetising, mouth-watering aroma that had appealed so much early in the day. Bacon sandwiches, the memories came flooding back of long days at the Yorkshire Show, the fast-food caravans were always a magnet when frying either onions or bacon, a deliberate ploy to entice those to move ever closer, the sirens' call to attack and hook victims by the nostrils instead of the ears. It seemed funny that when outside and the smell is carried on the breeze, the attraction appears so great. Lighting a scented candle, he cracked open the window and stared at the garden. It was orderly. A bluetit hung from the feeder, he watched the agile feeding ballet for a few moments before his attention turned to the charity bag neatly placed on the floor. It would be collected the following day and it would vanish in a van of identical bags.

His attention was distracted by the shuffling from within the metal cage set on the end of a worksurface. The small, honey-coloured creature ran within its wheel, almost hidden legs moving as fast as bees' wings, a blur. Collecting the empty toilet roll tube, he held it to his eye as if it were a microscope and watched the pet. The hamster stopped, moving across the cage to drink from the water bottle. It was always such a delicate process. As he opened the cage door, the creature scampered to its small plastic house and he popped the tube inside. It would only be moments before the curious ball of fur inspected the imposter. With constantly twitching nose it looked inside before darting and hiding briefly in the tube. "It doesn't take you long, Lord Byron. Like your ancestors." The words of the poem came to mind. "Those beastly Assyrians – '*The Assyrians came down like a wolf on the fold.*'" He quoted the part of the poem with force. "You're a curiously brave little fellow I'll give you that." He chuckled, turned to the sink, rinsed the milk bottle before drying his hands and collecting his coat. The bottle was deposited on the front step and he left the house. The hamster started to gnaw at the cardboard tube.

Chapter 5

The scooter was located more quickly than Owen could have hoped, it had been found parked on Providence Terrace. Owen looked at Harry Nixon, the expression said more than words could. "That's out of the way unless you live there. No shops or anything." He checked the address of the missing girl's boyfriend and pulled a face that showed confusion. "Is the scooter damaged?"

Harry shook his head. "On the contrary. The key was still in it or near it. No fuel, however. The house owner who reported it says it wasn't there at ten last night but there at seven this morning. They didn't hear it either and they're light sleepers."

"Empty, probably it was pushed there. Do any of the houses in the vicinity have CCTV?" Owen leaned forward, his fingers drummed the desk as if the action allowed the new information to sink in.

"Nope. According to her parents she hated riding in the dark so highly unlikely she drove or shoved it there at that time. The bike's been collected and Forensics will see what can be gleaned, providing the rain last night didn't eradicate what evidence there might be. He gives with one hand and takes away with the other. Such is the life of a copper!" Nixon looked towards the ceiling and turned to go.

That was the second religious quote Owen had heard that morning and he wondered if policing today's crimes now needed divine intervention. Picking up the phone he called April.

"Does a girl get no peace. Day off, it's on the rota." April feigned anger then laughed. She was always happy to chat with Owen.

"Sorry to sound thick but Cyril said he was going to ask you to have a word about a road to Damascus. He was mumbling about darkness into light. You've heard about the missing girl?" From the traffic noise he could tell she was out and he assumed she would be walking her dog on The Stray.

"Yes, I heard. Any news?"

"We found her scooter, a Vespa, and miraculously it's intact including the key!"

"That's a positive step, usually they've faced a fiery end or they vanish completely. And Owen, about Damascus, you'll need to read Acts 9 and if my memory serves me well, verses one to nineteen. A blind man sees." She heard Owen chuckle. "Has something dawned?"

"I understand what he was getting at, thanks. Talks in bloody riddles some mornings that man. That's probably what makes him good at his job. Thinks differently from most. What do they say these days, thinks outside the box?"

She chuckled. "You'll not hear that from me I can assure you of that, hate the saying. Makes me feel quite claustrophobic for some reason. How's the babe?"

"Like his dad, handsome and well behaved, thanks, April. See you tomorrow?"

"Eats and sleeps more like! Indeed, you will."

***

The preliminary Forensics report had returned that the fingerprints on the Vespa were those of the girl, Vance, those of her boyfriend and her father. There were others but as yet these were unidentified. There was also superficial damage but that was thought to have happened in the initial week of ownership owing to her inexperience. There were also some scratches and indentations as well as yellow paint to one side and the brake lever was bent. No explanation about that could be given. Checking the additional attached notes confirmed to Owen that the immediate door to door enquiries had been completed but without success. Final checks were still needed. He looked away from the computer screen.

"To date, nobody on the road knew the girl, recalled seeing the scooter before nor were admitting to it," he mumbled to himself. Turning back to the screen Owen checked the list of the property owners' names and those living close by. He decided to have a further check carried out; a wider sweep. Something did not sit right. He took another look at the list. It was not unusual for houses to be missed as some occupants might have been at work. However, official notes were left for occupiers requesting they contact the police with any information.

Owen checked his phone. There was a text from Brian Smirthwaite, according to the cafe owner, Sadie did not go into work.

***

Sadie Vance came to and felt the heat. The ache in her neck and to the side of her head was intense. Her memory

25

was hazy. She knew neither where she was nor why. Instinctively she moved a hand but it seemed locked above her with only the narrowest of movement available. Her body felt sticky and she could smell the acrid aroma of warm, stale sweat. She appeared to be neither standing nor lying down but in a semi-vertical position. It might have been the throb in her head that brought a sense of disorientation. Nothing touched her feet until she moved them and that was only a short distance before they brushed a hard, curved surface to the front and behind her. Where were her shoes? Her feet and legs were bare, her naked arms drawn above her head like those of a diver and her hands rested on a smooth, inner surface.

Looking up along their length she could only see what appeared to be a gauze or finely woven material over a circular opening that allowed the light to penetrate just beyond her finger tips. She tried banging on the dull, inner grey surface but was rewarded only with a barely audible thud. The rest of her body seemed trapped, confined, tight, allowing her very limited movement. Her confused mind had already begun to play cruel tricks and she started to hyperventilate fearing an asthma attack would be triggered. She tried to relax and keep control as she had been instructed as a child. She needed to comprehend where she was. There was a smell, familiar with that of the cafe – bacon – yes, she inhaled slowly through her nose. 'Am I dreaming or dead?' she thought, moving her head as much as possible, trying to bring as many senses into play without aggravating the throbbing pain. 'Surely not. I can smell, hear, feel, touch and see.' She closed her eyes and tried to remember. 'The church, the car and the person in the road.' It was a blur, as if in a dream.

Her initial memory on waking and finding herself in this position was one of panic. Above the pain she had struggled to free herself but quickly feeling the compressing force bred a claustrophobic anxiety, an entrapment that induced fear. Her breathing grew more rapid and animalistic noises erupted from within her throat. She tried to move, twist and squirm in order to release herself but she was stuck fast. With great determination and courage, she had managed to bring her fear and therefore her breathing under control realising the futility of any further struggle.

She had felt the need to pee and had held out until she could hold no longer. The urine had come and warmed her inner thighs before running off her toes. She had cried but nobody had heard. There was no real sound, she seemed to only hear her own heartbeat. Holding her breath, she listened. There was silence, thick and treacly like she had never experienced before, but it was then, from within that deep viscosity of inaudible blackness, she heard a familiar noise: the sound of a car horn somewhere in the distance, faint but familiar. Her face flushed and a smile of hope came to her lips for the first time. It confirmed she was not dead.

Chapter 6

The paperwork was slowly being tamed. It was the worst work element for Cyril but a necessary part of the job. "Administration!" He allowed the word to slip from his tongue with a good deal of disdain, one syllable at a time. The term paperwork, however, was a misnomer as most tasks were now completed on screen. It had taken him longer than most to come to terms with working digitally. Pausing, he thought of the old sweats who must have bemoaned the removal of typewriters as new technology was introduced. Carbon paper, Tipp-Ex, the ring of the bell, the Pavlovian signal indicating the need to start a new line, all came to mind.

He was not old enough to have used them professionally but he remembered his father sitting at his desk with the Olivetti Traveller typewriter before him. He had watched as his father's fingers danced on the keys; to a young child they were a blur. The click of the keys striking the paper was almost rhythmical. He recalled the chrome arm to the left of the machine being snatched allowing the upward movement of the paper and the start of a new line. The instrument seemed alive, the tapping, the click of the ratchet as the paper was drawn through was the heartbeat and on completion of the line the ring of the bell, that bell –

he could still hear it, it's tone sharp and instructional.

He remembered the first time he had typed, his father guiding his fingers to spell out his name. Smiling to himself Cyril looked at the mouse and the keyboard before him. Now there was silence, accuracy and variety – 'the computer is soulless! Speed! Don't forget speed and efficiency'. His thoughts ran ahead. If he were honest, he still preferred paper over screen, but the projector and the computer systems within the briefing room allowed for greater flexibility and it was with what the team was now familiar.

April tapped on the door. Cyril turned, smiled a welcome before pointing to the chair.

"Ever use a typewriter, April?"

Taken aback she clutched some papers to her chest allowing the question to sink in. "Went to a wedding last year and at the reception they had a variety of machines with paper and envelopes. There was a request for the guests to type a message to the happy couple. The younger guests present, those under forty, struggled with inserting paper and changing lines. The grandparents were in their element demonstrating how to use them. Once they'd mastered it you couldn't get them off them. I believe many bought old machines after that experience. They were a real novelty."

"It's funny how we soon forget. I wonder how many typewriters have been thrown out, having become obsolete?" His demeanour changed and he shook his head. "They were everywhere, in every office and typing pool. You wouldn't remember those I suppose, goodness, I hardly do in reality."

"Sounds like a sweat shop!" April smiled. "Mind, when we have a computer issue or power failure, we might wish we still had a couple." She paused allowing Cyril his moment of nostalgia. "If we may travel to the present, we have the ANPR records of Vance's scooter."

"And?"

"When working the girl took the same route to and from the cafe. There were anomalies within that routine but we've run them past her parents and boyfriend. There were a couple, however, to which we don't have answers. The day she went missing we know she didn't turn up for work but she'd have to travel this route to get to her home and it was closed. A water burst caused a flooded road necessitating a diversion. For a scooter rider she had a number of options to circumvent the problem." She opened the file and brought out an enlarged street map. "I've marked possible routes and also the locations including her home, work and the site where the scooter was found. There are five alternative ways if she stayed riding. We doubt she pushed it."

"Time differences? And was she expected home?" Cyril followed the routes marked in different coloured highlighter ink.

"Yes. She was going out with her boyfriend that evening but the date didn't happen as he received a text cancelling."

"Have you looked for public CCTV on all routes and requested dashcam footage?" Cyril sat back interlocking his fingers.

April nodded and he knew that all the basic police procedures would have been followed. Missing persons was considered in all cases to be a serious crime until proved otherwise. Time was critical, the golden hour rule was adhered to, providing they were notified swiftly. "The initial investigating officer's risk assessment and process was sound. We have, as you know, photographs and a DNA sample of the missing girl." She stared at Cyril before continuing. "The parents are also receiving professional support. One other thing, she suffers from asthma, uses Albuterol, Ventolin to you and me. Her attacks aren't frequent now but they've been known to be severe."

***

Lifting his arm, he brought the fabric of his jacket sleeve to his nose. Even after being outside for fifteen minutes, the smell from the bacon he had fried earlier still lingered. Maybe it was the accumulation of many identical morning meals. The day was fine. Not surprisingly, the road blocked the previous day was no longer closed and temporary traffic lights filtered the lines of vehicles. Work still progressed within the excavated piece of Tarmac. A visit to the bank, to buy a coffee and return home were all he had planned for the morning, if the need for some time to reflect was discarded.

Sitting on the bench to the edge of The Stray, the coffee, *to go,* warmed his hands, he observed a scooter negotiate the stationary cars, eager to reach the front of the queue. The sight made him flush with an uncontrollable excitement and his thoughts turned to the girl. She had mumbled about a scooter, had even carried a crash helmet. "You must take opportunities just like the Assyrians did, as they come to you, seize the moments as they are often few and far between. The weaker sex …" he emphasised the word *weaker* almost spitting out the two syllables.

"Controlling and manipulative, hiding their incompetence with a smile or a demeanour that's false. Their mask of Janus, faces to suit all occasions that are created to pull the wool over the faces of others. Why was I the only one who saw this?"

He sipped his coffee, the sweetness improving his mood. It was then a fear struck him. The true implications of his actions flooded his conscience as the scooter at the roadside revved and pulled away. Closing his eyes, he replayed the moment the girl had sought help, she would have taken any assistance she could. It was spontaneous, a gift and he had accepted it with open arms.

Chapter 7

The cafe was busy, the large window facing the street was opaque with condensation. A child, sitting close to the glass, had doodled faces in the moisture generating downward streams of water that moved like growing vertical snail trails. It was the smell that attracted Owen as he moved towards the counter and he felt more hungry than usual.

"Find a seat and I'll be with you in a minute." The girl's welcome was warm if a little fractious but she had smiled before turning to tap the coffee grounds from the filter handle into a metal lined bin.

Leaning over the counter he checked his notes. "I'm here to see a … Lindsey Aitchison, the owner. I'm Detective Inspector Owen." He had difficulty reading his own writing.

"She's in the back preparing an order. She'll be a minute I'm afraid. Sorry, busy time. One of your chaps was in yesterday." She turned the lever on the machine and steam rose, the loud hiss drowning the end of her sentence. "Hope you're bringing good news about our Sadie." Her optimistic tone was clearly contradicted by the intonation.

Owen had read Brian Smirthwaite's report but needed greater clarification on two points. Lindsey came from the kitchen, checked the order sheet and moved to the table near the window. The child stopped drawing and wiped his wet hands on his upper jacket sleeves. On returning to the counter, she spoke with her assistant, looked across at Owen, before walking over to his table.

Owen stood knocking the menu card onto the floor and causing the salt shaker to fall and spill some of its contents.

"Sorry, long legs, always a problem. Thanks for seeing me."

She looked at the spilt salt. "A few grains over your left shoulder is customary," she said with sincere instruction and followed her own advice. "Good news about ...?" Lindsey looked directly up at Owen, a degree of hope in her eyes.

"She's still missing, sorry to say. We're doing what we can. Can we talk? Five minutes?"

Lindsey turned to her assistant and held up her hand and mouthed, *five minutes.*

"I believe, from your chat yesterday, you received a text from Sadie to say she wouldn't be in work."

"I did. It was brief. Menstrual cramps which sounded strange, not at all like her." She pulled a face. "She usually said period pains and added some expletives."
Owen made a note. "Has she called in before with this problem?"

"A couple of times, problem with the pill she said ... you know or maybe you don't. She had particularly heavy periods. She also suffers occasionally from asthma but she self-medicates so there's rarely a problem. She's a good kid."

Owen felt a little uncomfortable as he made a note. "You gave my colleague a list of customers who were regulars. You mentioned also that one or two from the list seemed to have taken a shine to Sadie." He paused hoping that she would see where his enquiry was leading. "Could you specify those from this list?" Placing the notepad on the table she sat allowing her finger to run down the column.

"Pretty girls with a bubbly personality attract a certain type of customer but this is a cafe and not a pub. Most I'm sure just liked her joie de vivre." She looked back at the names. "This one always wanted to be served by her and always left a generous tip and then there was Rosie Snodgrass, Snodgrass, I kid you not. Lovely old dear. She always made a great fuss of Sadie." She continued down the list. "Ah! Frank." She tapped the page. "Never discovered his last name. Looked older than his years is my impression. They were like the lady and the tramp when together. He always seemed scruffy, he shaved but he didn't if you get my meaning. He appeared to have missed large areas; seemed to sprout in clumps and worst of all, his flies were seldom done up. I told him once to save his embarrassment but he announced that a dead bird can't fall from its nest!" She blushed as she laughed. "We get all kinds in here. That's about it if you don't count her boyfriend and her sister."

"This Frank, has he been coming here long?"

"Couple of months, maybe longer. We don't take a register, Inspector. Same order every time, sits in the corner over there and reads, poetry, I think that's what I saw. He's obviously an educated man. Coffee and a toasted teacake every time. Always mentions the smell of the bacon but never orders it."

"Has Sadie had any trouble with him or other customers

recently? Maybe wrong order or …?" He let the rest of the question hang.

There was a long pause, her face wrinkled into a frown. "There was one, last week. I heard about it after the event. A customer was unhappy with his latte, said it was cold and although Sadie brought a fresh cup, he tipped it on the floor. Refused to pay and became rather obnoxious, awkward, loud like. His language, shall we say, was rather ripe. Sounded like a total misogynist if you want my opinion. That was until Tom stepped in."

"Tom?"

"Tom Ward, he's on your list – there." She looked and pointed to the paper." A regular. Big lad, a bit like you. According to Stef there," she then pointed to the girl behind the counter, "Tom went over, moved Sadie behind him and whispered in the bloke's ear."

"And?"

"Let's just say he didn't leave without apologising and paying."

"Had Stef seen him before or since?"

"I know she'd not seen him before, I asked her and Sadie that very question. You get various grades of upset but I suggest to my staff that the customer is usually right to save any trouble but he was definitely out of order. Only wish I'd been here. Haven't seen Tom since either. I also asked them to describe the nowty sod but he seemed like Mr Average. Strange thing, he was well dressed and his behaviour seemed totally out of character but I guess you can't judge a book by the cover. Usually at times like that you're not aware of what the person looks like, you're just trying to sort the problem as quickly as possible."

"No CCTV?" Owen asked almost knowing the answer.

"It's a cafe!"

"How do I find Tom?"

"As I say, he's a regular and when he's in I could ask him to call you, Inspector ...?"

"Owen. That would be a real help. Ask your staff again for a description of the trouble maker and if anything comes to mind, I'd be grateful. In cases like this the smallest piece of information can make the biggest difference."

"It's getting worrying, Inspector Owen, she's no longer absent, more like disappeared and we know the usual outcome when pretty girls disappear." She picked up the menu card and turned it over. "We've added her photograph onto these in the hope someone might see her and report the sighting. We've asked them to ring 999. Hope that's alright?"

"Thanks. The more people looking for her the better."

"One more thing, but I'm not sure ..." Lindsey frowned and took a quick look at the queue forming at the counter. Stef tapped her wrist before raising her hands. Three people had come in adding to the need for service. Fortunately, Owen's mobile rang. It was DC Stuart Park. Lindsey's sentence was left unfinished.

Owen smiled. "I've taken too much of your time, you're certainly busy." He thanked Lindsey and moved outside keeping the phone to his ear. "Problem?"

"We've a mother at the station with her son. It's about the scooter. It seems as though he found the bike yesterday evening leaning against a skip in Cambridge Terrace. Thought it was junk." He paused to let the incredulity of the excuse sink in. "Apparently, his mother saw him pushing the bike and he told her originally that he was helping a friend. She'd believed him until she heard your report on the local news about the girl's scooter. It was then his story changed and he told her he found it."

"How old is he?" Owen had heard many excuses but he had to admire the lad's creativity.

"Eighteen and according to mum he's not the sharpest tool in the box. Her words."

"What time was he home?"

"I'll need to check that."

***

Sadie's legs seemed numb, the constraint against her upper body appeared to occlude the blood flow to her shoulder and lower limbs before the paresthesia began to aggravate and dominate her thoughts.

"Somebody, please help me." Her weakened voice barely echoed within the encapsulating space. She let her head fall forward until it rested between her upward stretched arms. For the first time she heard a noise, it was close, just beyond the upper opening. Her senses burned, alert to the slightest sound. Lifting her face, the mesh-covered opening now became a circle of hope. "Help! Anyone!"

"You want to be born again? Is that what you want?" The voice was calm, the words dripped with a gentleness that gave her a feeling of optimism yet somehow the question seemed rhetorical, as if not directed at her. She felt as if an answer would be an insult for stating the obvious.

"Yes, yes please. I'm hurting and scared. Please! I need my inhaler." It was almost a whisper as the tears flowed

38

spontaneously. The words came in spurts along with her breathing, it was uncontrolled and eager, maybe too eager and too quiet to receive any real response.

Within seconds, the light grew dim. She sensed the opening at the base below her feet suddenly becoming closed, sealed. There was a squeak as if something was forced into the opening. She tried everything to move but her naked skin seemed glued to the sides of whatever held her. It tore in places bringing a searing pain and an immediate desire to cease further exertions. She concentrated on the circle above, the only source of light. A silhouetted head partially blocked that light, any clarity denuded by the skin-like gauze covering and her developing tears.

"After light comes darkness. It always does and always will. Good night and as my mother would say, 'Don't let the bedbugs bite', then she'd close the door and the world would just carry on – talking, the strange and different voices. Then there were the grunts and the groans and often the screams. No faces you understand, there were never faces. I remember the blackout curtains – no light. I liked that, I think Lord Byron likes it too as he's always hiding, shuffling and snuffling. There's something reassuring about the dark, don't you think? It wraps you and protects you. The cloak of invisibility I used to call it. Anyway, nostalgia never pays. Must get on."

What appeared to be a black cover was fitted with the same squeak as a plastic surface was forced within the opening ring. It seemed to immediately suck the remaining light, leaving a heavy blackness that was thick, suffocating and menacing, not at all like he had just described the darkness. A strong smell of contact adhesive now stabbed her nostrils. It seemed to terminate the hope she had clung on to. Her now desperate screams only seemed to bring greater torment.

Chapter 8

The report about the missing girl within the national newspapers seemed to be an insignificant comment on the society of the day and like the girl, it was lost amongst the other column inches. It was almost an irrelevance, but closer to home, the local media had a greater focus. Owen's rather clumsy presentation to camera proved to be particularly poignant. Standing next to Sadie's sister, Blanche Vance, he spoke with emotional clarity and heartfelt words as he emphasised the personality and character of the girl for whom they searched. April felt her stomach flutter at the stoicism the youngster demonstrated as she addressed the camera at such a difficult and emotional time. Her pleas were not only sincere and unrehearsed, but very personal.

Within a short time of the interview going live, those manning the dedicated phone lines received details of possible sightings. Each call was logged and assessed. In the first two hours there were four calls purporting to be from the missing girl herself. There was a good deal of filtering to be done but on the other hand nothing would be allowed to slip through the net, no matter how bizarre the content of the call.

As Owen had mentioned in his address to the public, a

mobile police unit had been positioned within the centre of Harrogate. Posters of the girl adorned both sides of the vehicle in the hope of attracting and jogging the public's memory. An Incident Room had been established. Images of the girl and the scooter were displayed alongside a street map detailing the incoming sightings. The number of reports continued to grow. Captured dashcam footage was broken down and the routes highlighted on the map. The recent information of the initial location of the scooter corresponded with one of the routes determined by April to be an alternative way home. It also happened to be the most isolated.

Shakti stood with Harry Nixon.

"She could have just buggered off. Teenagers often feel the world is going too slowly or owes them a living. Maybe she was even tempted by the promise of a little excitement." His words seemed inappropriate and callous.

"Maybe she's just been snatched." There was a bitterness in Shakti's tone. "Two hundred and fifty-five people are still missing in all of Yorkshire and their fate is unknown. Seventy-four of those are children. Harry, concentrate on the words – 'fate unknown'. On our patch alone we're still looking for thirty-six in that situation, their loved ones are constantly living a nightmare." She paused in the hope the statistics would temper his attitude. It did not. "Seven of those are kids. Their whereabouts are unknown, taken maybe, dead, delivered as living sex toys, slaves. Now we have Sadie Vance, vanished, disappeared as if by magic. According to her parents and sister, she's a happy girl with much to live for and you stand here and think she's just 'buggered off' for a bit of fun?" Her tone grew more passionate. "That's what's wrong with policing today, there's no empathy, no urgency, just hard-faced seasoned, old coppers who send each other WhatsApp messages and rude, inappropriate jokes."

"Less of the old!"

Shakti sighed deeply. "There are no signs or evidence of mental illness, a major contributing factor in many disappearances. Sadie has a steady job, a loving family and a caring relationship and you want me to believe it's because, *the world is going too slowly!*" The cynicism within her tone did not go unnoticed.

Harry raised his eyebrows, that was not his only protest.

"Did you know that Humberside has the most unsolved missing person cases and do you know why that is, Shakti?" He did not turn to face her.

She shook her head. "Maybe it's because it's a port and you can skip to Europe in the back of a truck." She sounded neither convinced nor comfortable with her answer.

"Because of the Humber Bridge. A case of *Goodnight Vienna* and over you go to disappear forever, washed out to sea and that's if your body stays in one piece after hitting the water from such a height. You think valuable police resources should be available for however long it takes to find them?"

Shakti pulled a face displaying her disgust at the thought. "Some of those have been forced onto the bloody boats, trafficked. Many disappearances are not crimes, foul play's not in the game. However, we should remember a very small percentage of disappearances are planned, cruel and sinister. Kidnap, the victim is moved into the underworld and we know for what. Trapped and imprisoned in the claustrophobic and lost world of pure evil, a place where the victims are but pawns. Weigh up the evidence, she works in the public eye. She's beautiful, vivacious and young. Did you ever see the film, 'Taken'?" She turned and looked at her colleague.

"Yes. 'I will find you and I will kill you', great line. They brought out Taken 2 and 3."

She wanted to hit him.

"Women are less likely to go missing than men but when they do, think of the cases that are still left unsolved, left open and to quote you, their fate unknown. Will they ever be found?" He answered his own question rapidly. "No. If you don't find them in a set time ..." He raised his shoulders to punctuate the end of the sentence. "There's every chance you'll find the body sometime down the line. Remember, trafficking is a two-way process."

The more Shakti considered his idea, fuelled by the memory of the film, she could certainly see his point and a tingle of cold fear rippled along the nape of her neck.

"For your interest I don't have WhatsApp and therefore neither do I send or receive inappropriate messages and jokes. Just wanted you to be clear."

Shakti placed her hand on his shoulder and whispered the word, 'Sorry.'

***

April sat alongside DC Dan Grimshaw. The atmosphere in the room was to be expected. John Thompson sat between his parents and it was clear from the shadows beneath his eyes he had been deeply affected by his girlfriend's disappearance.

April spoke first after reassuring all concerned that they

were doing everything they could to locate Sadie. "I know we've talked before but I also know the initial shock may have clouded your thoughts. On our previous visit I asked you to reflect on the last few weeks, to consider those places where you've been together and the people you might have met and to make a written record of those reflections. Did you do that?"

John nodded and pointed to the notebook on the coffee table.

"May I?" April leaned forward in anticipation. The notes were broken into date order detailing their meetings and a number of names involved. "You mainly drove or were driven by friends?"

"Yes, when I could have mum's car I drove. Sadie only used the scooter to go to work or come here and that was if the weather was fine. She didn't like the wet or the dark. She couldn't wait to pass her test and neither could I as she was not the best rider."

"We've received details of Sadie's last call out and that was to you but it didn't connect which suggests it was either cut off, the phone was damaged or the battery failed. We know she tended to text rather than phone. Did you receive the call?"

He nodded again. "It rang twice, maybe three times and by the time I'd found the phone there was nothing other than a missed call. I tried calling back but there was nothing, not even an engaged tone."

"Were you concerned?"

"I thought she might have to cancel our evening together, but no, not really, it happens. Some areas have crap coverage. Only when I was about to call her before we were due to meet did I worry. I received the text saying she couldn't make it and we would chat later." He found the text on his phone and handed it to Dan Grimshaw.

"This was her?" Dan handed the phone to April.

"There was no kiss at the end and that was unusual."

"Her mother was sent a similar text saying she was staying at yours and would see them after work the following day."

"There's no easy way of asking this, John, but could she have been seeing someone else?"

John wrapped his arms around himself and allowed the question to sink in.

"Boyfriend? Relationship?"

John mumbled as if struggling with a fact that he was not prepared to accept.

It was April's turn to nod.

His face conveyed a degree of confusion. The silence was now palpable. "I don't know. I sometimes had a suspicion that she was seeing someone else. She'd cancel a date at the last minute and when I asked her about it, I was told that I was too possessive and we'd have a row. I'd then feel stupid as I'd spoiled the evening. That's why I didn't make a fuss this time."

"Did you discuss this with your mutual friends?"

"No. We'd not see each other for days after the row. I'd text an apology and hear nothing and then she'd call as if nothing had happened. Sometimes I don't think I'll ever understand the workings of the female mind."

Grimshaw breathed out audibly. Even at his age and with one failed marriage behind him he still had not discovered the secret.

"You know she called in work sick. Didn't go in the day she went missing?"

"Ill? Her asthma?"

"Period discomfort."

"She never had problems with … She wasn't on her period." His faced flushed as he looked at his mother and then back at April. "Do you think she's alright?" The sentence was fractured as John began to break down.

Neither April nor Dan answered the question directly. "There are a lot of people looking out for your girlfriend as we sit here." She placed a hand on his shoulder. "People can just take off, need space to sort out their thoughts and what they want. Youth can get very confusing. We must have faith. May I keep this?" She held up the note pad.

He nodded. "You will find her?"

"We'll do everything possible. You have my word."

The rain was falling as the officers left the house; large, heavy droplets as if the heavens were about to split and spill their contents. The spots peppered the pavement as they dashed to the car. The sound was amplified once inside as the rain turned to hail. Deep, grey clouds spread as far as the eye could see.

"You can understand the confusion. Why she wasn't considered missing for over twenty-four hours. The texts told conflicting stories."

"The texts tell lies. Words without faces to back them up."

"The last call, the text sent from somewhere near Thruscross Reservoir, miles out of the way. Surprised there was a signal. Although I didn't say so in there, the phone was switched off not battery failure. We know that because the tech people have informed me that simple action sends a certain identifiable pulse."

"That's why they're known as smart phones. The world can track you if it has half a mind. Your personal life is not your own."

Chapter 9

Pauline Guy sat a distance from her son as if the anger and the threat of severe chastisement was ever present. Carl's head hung low as he played nervously with his hands. Owen entered with Dr Helen Knowles, a psychologist attached to the family liaison unit and linked with the youth justice offending team. He placed the electronic tablet on the table before looking primarily at the lad. Carl did not respond.

"This interview will be recorded, Carl, for your benefit as much as ours. My colleague cautioned you when you arrived so you must be under no illusion about the seriousness of the situation." He looked at Carl Guy but the young man did not return his gaze. "This is Dr Knowles, she's here to help you and your mum. From our records you've not been in trouble before. Now, tell us about the scooter."

There was a long pause, the silence hung and the sounds from outside the room seemed amplified. Owen stared at the young man but saw the demeanour of a child. He let the flat of his hand fall on the table, the slap was loud, making Carl jump. "We're here because of you and your actions, lad, actions that could be very serious indeed. We need to know everything." He leaned forward and raised a finger on the hand that had brought a focus to the proceedings. "And everything you say must be the truth, the whole truth."

His mother pushed a hand into his side. "Are you listening?" Her words were sharp as flecks of spittle accompanied the question. He nodded. Knowles said nothing but noted the lad's responses, both non-verbal and physical.

"The scooter was where I said, that road that leads from near Betty's cafe." He turned to his mother, a look of confusion clearly visible.

"Cambridge Terrace," she smiled as if to give encouragement.

He nodded. "Yes, there. It was by a skip, leaning against it like. It wasn't on its stand and one of the lever things was bent as if it had fallen. I looked about but there was no one. Even walked round the skip as there was a lot of other stuff, builders' stuff like. It was there I saw the keys. They had a heart shape for a key ring. I didn't know they'd fit until I tried and it started. I covered the number plate with a piece of cement bag, tied it in a knot like and rode it." He turned again to his mother and then back at Owen. All the while he played with his fingers. "I didn't do it on purpose, steal it like. Thought it was dumped. Honest!"

"Where did you ride it?" Owen asked adding notes into the electronic tablet as he spoke.

"I'd no thingy," he pointed to his head.

"Helmet," his mother added.

"Helmet, yes, crash helmet so only round the back streets away from the main roads but it ran out of petrol. I pushed it down the road next to the graveyard. And left it."

"What time was that?" Owen looked directly at the boy who swiftly turned towards his mother.

"I saw Carl at about 7.15."

Carl raised his shoulders and nodded in agreement.

"Were you wearing gloves?" Owen let the question hang as if it was the least important.

He nodded again.

"You need to speak, Carl!" His mother's tone was sharp and impatient.

"I found some of them blue ones, doctor type gloves in the skip. I used them as I've seen them do that on the telly, finger prints and stuff. I dumped them in the grass when I climbed into the graveyard. I needed to get home but when me mum came in, she asked what I'd been doing with the scooter. I lied. I'm sorry. I didn't think anyone wanted it as it was by the skip." He looked frantically at the adults in turn. There was clear fear in his voice. "I told her it belonged to a friend." His eyes shifted to his mother.

"The heart on the key ring. What happened to it?"

Carl frowned. "I chucked it. Pulled it off. 'I love you', it said." He pulled a face showing his distaste.

"Skip?"

"Yes."

His mother let her left arm sweep across and she clipped the back of his head. "What have me and your dad told you about taking stuff?"

Owen raised a hand but said nothing to her. He continued to talk to the lad. "You've made a difficult situation worse. You know that? Think carefully before you answer. Did you see anyone else near the scooter?"

Carl rubbed the back of his head. "No, but I saw a car. It

51

came out just before I went into the terrace. I was up by the bank."

"Colour? Make?" Owen sat up.

"Black or dark blue ... not sure. Never been into cars, sorry."

The anti-climax made Owen's shoulders fall. If he did not know the make, he would probably have seen little else but he had to ask. "Was there a passenger?"

"No, I don't remember seeing one. I'd just finished work, I was later than I hoped as I'd been helping move some furniture, maybe six o'clock. Don't have a watch, use my phone. Never good with watches. Get confused. Ask mum, she knows."

Owen looked at the notes. "Hotel work?"

"Help out in the one at the bottom of Montpellier, The Crown. I've done it since leaving school. I love it." He paused. "I'm so sorry. Will I lose my job? I can't lose it." He began to weep. His mother leaned forward and wrapped her arm around his shoulders.

Owen stood and signalled to Dr Knowles. "We'll leave it there. I'll need to see you again, Carl, but for now you need to be in work." It was understood from the records and the conversation with Pauline Guy, his mother, that he had learning difficulties and any success had been through supportive home and school co-operation. As far as Owen and Dr Knowles were concerned, he would be trusted to the Youth Outcomes Panel but they both felt that no further action other than family support would be needed. It was considered critical that he be allowed to maintain a stable job, at a place he enjoyed and in which he felt safe. For Carl Guy, they believed a lesson had been learned. The formality of the process would be enough and they hoped they would, along with the Family Liaison Unit, have done enough to prevent further misdemeanours.

Owen requested a check of the skip for the missing heart-shaped key ring attachment.

***

Owen sat at his desk after leaving the interview. Dr Knowles would now instigate the next stage of the procedure. He slipped his hands behind his head and stared at the photograph of his son. He had just witnessed the full spectrum of parental emotions within a twenty-minute period. The path of parenthood was paved with many different and at times difficult emotions. He knew a degree of leniency would be shown to help protect the lad, who had, he felt, learned a valuable lesson.

Reading Owen's mood, Shakti quietly approached Owen's desk. "I've looked at the lad's notes. He had made an error. We all do. The skip has gone but we've contacted the owner and they say it's not been sorted yet. It's painted yellow so the paint on the scooter is probably a match. I've sent someone round to get a scraping and to find the missing heart. There's no CCTV near but we're checking the camera at the top of Parliament Street, The Ginnel and the junction of King's Road. We're going from half an hour either side of Carl's timing. The car could only go two ways."

"Unless the scooter had been there longer. Find out when the builders clocked off, Shak, and see if it was there when they left. Also contact Forensics and check if the yellow paint is definitely from the skip."

Owen looked at his watch, a watch that once belonged

to his boss. He considered the time from when the girl first went missing. It was not looking positive. He organised a briefing for the following morning. Hopefully they would have more information on which to build the search. He needed to chat with Carruthers, the search advisor.

***

The house was quiet. Removing his coat, he placed it on a hanger and hung it in the cupboard by the front door before moving into the lounge. The net curtains diffused the light. The room was ordered. Paintings, original oils, hung on most walls apart from one that contained a full row of book shelves. He had seen the police request for help on the news and was surprised it had come so soon. He had read that the Stephen Lawrence enquiry had been the catalyst for a change in the way police forces viewed cases concerning missing persons.

The black plastic, corrugated, twinwall cylinder was positioned on the purpose made frame. It sat at an angle, a bit like the gadgets that held a wine bottle. Beneath the raised lower end was a sheet of plastic and some plumber's absorbent pads. They were really redundant once the lower cap had been fitted, but for safety, he left two down. You could never be too careful. He needed tea. Standing, he tapped on the cylinder's wall. Nothing came back. He grinned.

The hamster sat within its own *happy pet* willow tube, its nose just visible. The remnants of the card toilet roll centre was now fragmented across the bottom of the cage.

"She's safely in her tube and you, my little friend … You made light work of that cardboard, Lord Byron." He popped the switch on the kettle before putting his head close to the hamster's cage. "Tonight, Lord Byron, I shall move our guest to somewhere very safe and then it will be back to just the two of us for the time being."

Chapter 10

A scooter had been seen by those leaving the building site but it had not been near the skip. Neither workman took any notice of it and could not confirm if it had sustained any damage; neither were they sure of the colour. One even suggested it was a yellowy colour, possibly primrose.

"Maybe the lad is not telling the whole truth," Cyril muttered to Owen. "The fact that he decided to wear gloves suggests he knew what he was doing and that it was not leaning against any skip."

"The heart from the key ring was found as well as the gloves from the cemetery. Maybe our Carl knows more than he's telling. We'll be making another call, sir."

"I note that Sadie's mother knew nothing of her taking the day off work or having an excessive problem with her period on this occasion or previously."

"Nope, according to two reliable sources she never suffered. Rarely had a day off school. Healthy kid apart from asthma but the medication helped her overcome any problems."

Cyril stood and leaned with his elbow on the filing cabinet, maybe he was drawn there psychologically. "Either she or someone with her phone is manipulating the situation and that gives me grave cause for concern,

Owen." He tapped the metal top. "Do we have triangulation of the known position when the phone was activated?"

"We have an approximate location but it's out in the wilds near Thruscross Reservoir. We doubt it was her as she'd not venture so far."

"Do we have the ANPR records for the day she went missing?"

"I've checked but nothing's come up so far. We just know her regular route was blocked to traffic. We've requested public help with dash cam footage but as yet, that's drawn a blank. The longer we wait the less likely it will come in. I'm surprised as whilst driving you tend to notice scooters, loud and nipping in and out of the traffic."

"Put out another call, broaden the search area. Something is not stacking up."

***

Tom Ward waited in the entrance to Harrogate Police Station, holding the cafe's business card. On the reverse was written Owen's name and telephone number. Within five minutes the door at the far end of the reception area opened and Owen entered. His tie was lowered and the top button of his shirt undone, his lanyard was tucked in the shirt breast pocket. Lindsey was correct, Ward was indeed a big man.

"Mr Ward, I didn't expect you to call in, just ring but either way I'm grateful."

Ward stood and shook the hand Owen proffered. The handshake was mutually firm. They moved into what was known as the informal interview room, it allowed the interviewee hopefully to relax. Tom was asked to explain the confrontation that had taken place in the cafe.

"Sadie was bloody furious. I thought she was going to slap him. I had to step between them. She might be petite but she showed real spirit."

Here was another contradiction in people's perception. "So, you were preventing rather than protecting?"

"Preventing her from clocking him? Yes."

"Had you seen him before?"

"Man in a tweed suite. There are many in Harrogate. I couldn't honestly say."

"What did you actually say to him and Sadie?"

Ward looked a little sheepishly before he answered. "I told him he'd have two people slapping him unless he paid and left. I also said my slap would be much harder than Sadie's. He understood. I suggested he pay, apologise and leave. He tossed a tenner on the table, gave Sadie a venomous stare and left. He wasn't a happy chap. Sadie went into what I presume is the kitchen and I didn't see her again. I left shortly after. All I can say is that she was furious and I mean seriously pissed off."

"Had the chap gone when you went outside?"

"I didn't look to be honest."

***

"Error strewn texts, unidentifiable sender, inaccurate medical issues, girl not where she's supposed to be, questionable facts about the cafe incident, probable lies about finding the scooter. Something smells, April, and it ain't frying bacon." Owen tapped the whiteboard.

Brian Smirthwaite walked into the Incident Room. He held two pieces of paper. "We've received some dash cam footage of the scooter. It was seen turning off Skipton Road onto St John's Road." Brian moved to the computer. The footage appeared on the screen at the far end of the room. "Confirmed to be the morning of the day she went missing so this can't be Carl Guy riding." He lifted the second piece of paper but focused on the screen. "The way it's being ridden suggests a lack of confidence so more than likely the rider was the girl."

Owen and April moved over to the road map of Harrogate fixed to a wall. It was already marked with routes and sightings.

"What was she doing out there? It's nowhere near any of the other relevant locations."

"And now for the icing on the cake." Brian dropped the piece of paper onto the desk. "Worse still, our scooter finder, Carl Guy, didn't go into work this morning and his phone is switched off. He's also missing. His mother called in. She's rather anxious. Apparently, he didn't go into work after the interview here. He went into his room and refused to budge but promised he'd go in today." He pulled a face feigning surprise. "She believes he might have done a runner, fearful of getting into trouble and losing his job if the officer came to interview him again. He admitted he'd lied about the scooter being found where he originally stated."

Owen looked at April and raised his eyebrows. "Never bloody rains but it pours in this job."

***

Carl Guy's mother sat on the settee. "I'm sorry, sorry!" Lifting her head, she looked at April. "I've put him under too much pressure over the scooter. He could never cope, but he seemed better, more confident since his father left." There was a pause as she stared at the carpet. April gave her time. She knew the woman was in turmoil, guilt had swamped her emotions denuding her of clear thought and inner strength.

"Has he gone missing before?" April spoke quietly but firmly as she leaned towards her.

Pauline nodded and dabbed a tissue to her nose. "When his dad was here and he'd given him a roasting he'd retreat to his bedroom and then he'd hear us row. Jim, his dad, would slap me and then become ..." she paused. "Aroused. It was dreadful. I knew Carl could hear everything. He'd disappear for hours until things had calmed down. He knew when his dad would be at work. He worked nights in a bakery. Carl's not gone missing like this since Jimmy left."

"He's not gone, Mrs Guy, he's just not turned up for work. Talk me through today."

"He left about 7.30 as usual. He called up. I don't sleep too well so stay until he's gone, an old habit as Jimmy liked me to be in bed when he got home." She glanced briefly at April and raised her eyebrows. "It's what Jimmy wanted and what Jimmy wanted was what Jimmy ... anyway, sorry!" She brought the tissue to her nose. "Anyway, Carl goes early to the hotel. He should start at 9.00 but he helps a bit in the kitchen and they give him his breakfast and spoil him. He told me they make him feel special. He would then put on his hotel uniform. They do all the laundry of that. I remember the first time I saw him in it. I was so proud of him. He'd failed at most things in his life or maybe I should say we failed him, his dad and me. They've been good with my lad and he told me that he was so frightened he'd be sacked for his behaviour, taking the scooter. I heard him crying. It kills me, Inspector Richmond, it truly does."

"So, he didn't sound anxious when he left this morning?"

"No, and if the hotel hadn't called me, I'd be none the wiser."

April checked her watch, it was 11.33. "He's been missing for four hours. We're checking CCTV footage and officers are walking the route he would normally take to work. If he walked it regularly people will have seen him. I want you to remain here just in case he comes home. He's obviously psychologically upset. Guilt, as you know, can be quite the demon. If he does return ..." April did not need to finish the sentence.

Three people had seen Carl that morning. One, a waitress at Betty's cafe who saw him daily, had waved and received a response. CCTV at the top of Parliament Street had a clear image of him approaching the road. The time was logged at 07.50. He was less than five minutes away from The Crown Hotel.

April checked the street map, tagging Carl's route and highlighting the points of identification. Picking up the phone she called the hotel receiving the usual polite 'How may we help'. April explained her position and the present situation requesting they send someone who knew Carl to look outside. Although situated at the confluence of a number of roads, to the front of the hotel was a small low-walled car park, beyond that a large and busy roundabout and on the pavement between the two were positioned a number of benches. She hung up and waited. Within ten minutes her phone rang.

"Carl is here. He was sitting on the bench at the front of the hotel. He's very upset. Our manageress is with him. He wants to stay and is extremely apologetic."

April's sigh of relief was clearly audible; it was as she had suspected.

The brief call to Carl's mum brought much relief. "He's in good hands, Mrs Guy, and he wants to stay. It's understandable. If I might suggest you could have his favourite meal for him when he gets home. He may want to talk, but then again ... As far as we're concerned it's a positive outcome. Let's hope he's on the way up and you all can rebuild his confidence. The hotel staff have been wonderful and obviously care a great deal about your son."

April removed the notes from the Incident Room wall. *If all missing persons' enquiries could end so swiftly and positively*, she thought before glancing across at the notes on the opposite wall for that of the missing girl. There was nothing so simple, more a web of uncertainty and confusion.

***

"So why would a girl who's not the most confident of riders travel so far away from her regular route? Why send spurious text messages? Why miss work and why lie about her condition? What's the attraction?" Carruthers, the search organiser looked at both Cyril and Owen.

For a few moments Cyril said nothing as he looked at the street map allowing his finger to rest on the area. "A veritable warren, look. Once on St John's Road you've a choice of routes. Needle in a haystack comes to mind. Many of the houses are well established with some new build to the upper area here and here. It's a maze of routes that would allow someone trying to cover their tracks the opportunity to do so and if, as you say, they're not too confident a rider, this is the ideal place. I take it we've no further sightings?"

"No."

"The question is, why?" What's the end game?" Owen rubbed his chin and perched on the edge of a desk.

"The scooter was supposedly left here out of petrol in the late afternoon or early evening according to Carl; we don't have a specific time. The neighbour assures us it must have been after ten and before seven the following morning. Carl was quizzed by his mother that evening so it was before ten. So, thoughts?" Cyril let the question hang in the air.

"Either our witness made an error or the scooter was moved again after Carl had left it." Carruthers's answers were neither confident nor convincing.

***

The cradle on which the plastic cylinder sat was dismantled to be stashed away later, the charity bag containing the girl's clothes had been collected earlier. The estate car was parked, boot lid raised in readiness. The thoughts of old crime films came to mind as the body wrapped in a rug was carried from the murder scene and he chuckled out loud. "Progress has been made. Here we have the modern version."

The cylinder's rigidity would make lifting and carrying a dead weight far easier. He had experimented by filling the tube with bags of compost. Allowing it to rest and then fall onto his shoulder proved straightforward. Balancing and lifting were easier than he could have hoped. Out of sight it would be easy to dump.

Once the cylinder was in the car he tossed in the electric drill and bit set before throwing a travel blanket over them all. The day, although starting out bright had, as the forecast had predicted, deteriorated. The developing poor weather suited the task. He would travel early in the evening and then park until he was confident that he had a degree of privacy. He would take his book.

Chapter 11

Hannah staying at home was the second reward of having a child; the flat was now more of a home and Owen loved it. Hannah, however, was torn between the pleasure of being at home with Christopher and the longing to be back at work. It was a strange dichotomy she had not experienced before. She did not want to miss a moment of Christopher's development and yet she felt as though she needed the challenge work offered her mental wellbeing.

Owen greeted Hannah with a kiss and a squeeze. She looked tired. Christopher was asleep in the carry cot. Owen moved across, leaned in and kissed the child on the forehead, Christopher did not move. Owen stood for some time just staring.

"He's got your nose, you know that?" He moved back towards Hannah and let his finger rest gently on the tip of her nose. "It's a beautiful gift from a beautiful mother and woman."

The words coming from such a large and clumsy man seemed a contradiction. He kissed her forehead.

"I've made a lasagne and there's wine opened for you. Thank you for the sweet words. Shower and I'll have everything ready. He's like his dad, always hungry so I'll sort him too. I'll leave you the nappy as I know you enjoy that part of parenthood." She grinned and blew him a kiss.

It was true, he would do anything to be near, touching, holding the child. It was as if he had suddenly become whole.

"No sign of the missing girl?" Hannah sipped sparkling water and picked some lettuce from her side salad with her fingers.

"Bloody scares me. She's a young and pretty girl with everything going for her, contradictions all along the evidence path. We've considered suicide and even though it can't be ruled out we feel …"

"That would contradict the general findings and from what I've witnessed I would imagine emotional dystopia." Hannah's expression conveyed real concern.

Owen looked quizzical.

"An imagined state where they feel that there is a great deal of injustice in society. As an adolescent did you not feel that the world was a crap place to be, your dreams were not being achieved? Kids feel these things acutely. They can be embarrassed by their parents' actions or aspirations, ever conscious of their lack of achievements or even a fear of the failing environment the scientists keep banging on about. There's also the possibility that nowadays they all want instant fame and to be valued by their peers." She poured more wine for Owen. "That's before we start talking about today's social media pressures."

"Never felt things like that. Some injustice regarding families but I knew I was loved. Tried to please people in the hope I could make them happy."

Hannah slid her hand across the table and placed it on his. He had not changed. There was a stirring from the cot.

"Your son needs a new nappy," she grinned. "Try not to get the contents on your T-shirt, it's clean on and certainly not a good look!"

***

The traffic was almost clear on the stretch of moorland road. The gravel layby had been vacant on his arrival and he had been joined by no other cars, nor he hoped would he be as it was getting too late in the day. He had planned the location with great care; there were neither walls nor drainage ditches to either side but there was a steep slope that ran into a narrow valley. The slope was heavily grown with bracken. A number of mature but weather-gnarled trees grew along the far side as the slope climbed away for a considerable distance. There were no pathways just the occasional sheep grazing within the area.

He had left town much earlier and chosen the route meticulously. There was always a fear that the registration number would be picked up on a number of ANPR cameras. He had read that there was one camera for every twenty-seven miles of road. He would go early and return late along his planned route, knowing he should be secure.

The deep, red slash that ran along the western horizon had slowly bled away and the darkness had now taken full hold. He would read no more. Another hour and he would move on. Reclining his seat, he closed his eyes and contemplated the opportunity he had been given – there she was, confused, holding a crash helmet but there was no evidence of a bike. She was clearly in distress, a gift, handed to him as if on a plate. The recent memory was fresh and clear in his mind's eye. She seemed drunk, possibly ill. There was nobody about, even though it was broad daylight. Maybe it was her arrogance, her dismissal of his offer to help. Maybe it was her disdain. It was now of little consequence. Probably he would never know but cared little. The blow was perfect; to the right side of her head and she had fallen straight into his arms. It was strange how something so simple as a small yet strong cardboard tube could be so effective. Who would look at it and perceive it as a weapon?

***

April sat with Harry Nixon as they went through the photographs taken from John Thompson's phone.

"Bloody hell, you'd never believe such a small device could store this many! How many are there?"

"A lot! The tech people have been selective too so think yourself lucky. They only included photographs from two months before they got together." He grinned. "Remember before phone cameras and you had to carry the damn thing? Only took selective pictures and you had to take them to the chemist to get them developed and now with disposable digital they photograph what they're about to eat!"

April looked at him remembering Cyril's earlier conversation about typewriters but said nothing. Progress was not all it was cracked up to be.

"They've also popped them through some new tech, a type of facial recognition software which collates selected faces as well as the ones seen determined by the selection process. So, once, twice and so on. They can also select male and female but that's not as accurate as we hoped. It does go some way to speeding up the selection process."

Within thirty minutes they had identified the faces and placed them on a sliding scale. They would then need John to identify and name them. Once that was completed, they could begin arranging interviews. April checked the clock on the wall. "I've had enough. Have you seen the time? Ralph needs a run and I need a beer. Set up an appointment for John Thompson to come in but please make it sooner. Tomorrow early, say nine."

***

The road through Blubberhouses, the A59, was a main artery route leading to and from Harrogate, a two-lane twisting road that works its way through Kex Gill and over the moors. A year or two back, part of the road at one of the steepest sections collapsed into the valley causing major disruption. Emergency work was needed to secure the hillside from slipping onto the carriageway, something that was happening with greater frequency, as well as to repair the damage to the road. The groundwork team had left a temporary track cut into the steep slope they had used during the procedure. It was here he could park the car and bide his time. The only fear he had would be a passing police car. He knew that if he were spotted, the police would return. To be caught with the cylinder and therefore the dead girl would not only be foolish, it would be pure carelessness that would end it there and then.

At this location there were no street lights and with the decreasing number of passing cars came a degree of peace, but not necessarily security. Kex Gill looked as it had done for centuries. The moon, partly hidden by cloud

69

seemed to float and the poem by Alfred Noyes came into his mind. 'The moon was a ghostly galleon tossed upon cloudy seas.' Fortunately, the road was not a ribbon of moonlight and there would be neither highwayman nor police, he hoped. How apt that poem was. Sitting back, he slipped his hands behind his head and tried to recite the first verse. Much of it came to mind. He remembered his teacher mentioning the word 'alliteration'. As a child he liked the idea of writing snapping sounds and tongue twisters – "Peter Piper picked a peck of pickled peppers", he said out loud enunciating each word. He leaned over and looked at the covered cylinder. "And some, my dear, fell on deaf ears." It was just before midnight. The moon had sunk with little trace into the ghostly grey of cloud cover and a light drizzle had begun to mist the windscreen. The intensity of darkness would be his ally allowing the lights of approaching vehicles to be seen more easily from further away, warning beacons of their approach.

The slope of the land and the angle of the parked car made the removal of the tube easier than he had hoped. With little effort, he slipped one end onto the ground and raised it vertically. It stood like a wide, black pole just taller than his own height. Bending, he let it fall across his shoulder and balance before he straightened up. The slight breeze caused it to weathercock slightly but he soon found a firm footing. He checked the road for approaching lights in both directions. There was none. Conscious of his foot placement he approached the tarmac edge before checking again. He crossed stopping at the opposite low black and white barrier and stone wall. Beyond that the land fell away steeply. The heavy cloak of bracken grew darker the further his eyes scanned into the gorge that was lined with trees camouflaging the beck. Slipping the tube from his shoulder he placed it along the top of the wall. Still no lights approached. Beads of sweat broke from his forehead as he took a breath and calmed his nerves. With a firm push, the tube left the wall and landed four feet below just away from the base of the structure on the steepest of inclines. It soon gathered speed. He watched as it rolled, occasionally rising above the bracken. The only sound, the dull thud as it made contact, was clearly heard but the lush vegetation absorbed and cushioned most of that sound. Soon it was lost, the black plastic swallowed within the engulfing darkness that the steep valley side offered. There was silence. It would be in Hall Beck. He felt the breeze channelled down the Gill and his senses were invigorated. His nerves tingled momentarily. It was time to go. Back in the car he closed his eyes and the poem flooded his mind yet again as he mouthed the words – *Back, he spurred like a madman, shrieking a curse to the sky.* Suddenly the consequences of his actions became apparent in the isolated darkness. It had been easier than he had hoped. *The highwayman came riding ...* It was time for home.

Chapter 12

The dark sky viewed through the kitchen window was streaked through with shots of yellow, red and a deep orange. The clouds he had seen grow at midnight had now evaporated. The day would be as forecast, fine. The hamster spun within the wheel as if taking its morning constitutional, happy and secure in its own enclosed space, oblivious to the world beyond. The repetitive thrum was soothing to the ear. With the iron frame that held the tube containing the girl folded and stored away, the room seemed immediately larger.

"Until next time," he said in a whisper as the cupboard under the stairs was closed as if trapping the frame within its own cage. He locked the door.

'You were kind to her. You didn't molest her, torment her, personally frighten her. You could have done all of those things. You just righted wrongs.' He sipped the tea. Taking a deep breath, he felt an emptiness as if he were again alone. He knew however, other opportunities would come along. Today before the morning traffic increased, he needed to go back to the place to see if the tube was visible from the road. It should not be but once released to roll away, nature and luck played a key role. First, however, breakfast called. He took the bacon from the fridge and set the frying pan on the stove.

Before leaving he opened the tailgate and saw the drill, realising he had forgotten to put holes in the plastic; the idea was to allow nature in, to aid the decomposition of the body. As it was, it was now hermetically sealed and a delay to that process would be inevitable. If the tube were visible, he could climb down and drill the cylinder whilst it was in situ and if possible make it more visually secure. He so desperately hoped he would not have to risk that.

The A59 was busier than he imagined it would be. He was always surprised at the number of heavy wagons using the route. He needed to climb the hill away from Fewston and turn round at the top as if heading for West End before turning to descend. That way, on the run down if he slowed significantly, he would be in the perfect position to see the spot where he had released the tube. Only if absolutely necessary would he pull off the road at the only available spot, the track made by the engineers, the track he had used the night before. However, in the day time should a passing police patrol spot his vehicle it would be disastrous. That had to be a last resort.

As he approached the ruined building to the right of the road he slowed. There was no one behind. There was no sight of the black tube only marks within the foliage where it had rolled. He breathed a sigh of relief. He had done it. If it were discovered in a week or so he was not concerned. He knew, however, that that was highly unlikely. Now, the morning could only get better and he had another task to perform, one that was far less stressful.

***

John sat nervously and looked at the large flat screen on

one wall. Checking his Apple watch he was still optimistic she might make contact, but so far, he had been disappointed. He knew why he was in the soulless room. He only needed to identify faces found in his photographs the officer had told him but he still felt the flutter of nerves. The hidden, distant voices and what seemed like a constantly ringing phone added a tension he found discomforting. He knew he would see Sadie's laughing face staring back, a face captured in many of his photographs, and that thought brought upset and a degree of uncertainty. He was not alone, his father sat to his left. Harry Nixon and April entered, each carrying a file and the notebook. They explained the procedure and reminded John that he was still under caution for no other reason but to secure accurate evidence for the sake of Sadie's safe return.

As they progressed through the allotted photographs, a number of names were repeated but it was the isolated individuals and the people John could not name that intrigued Harry. Wherever possible contact details were added to the names.

***

Turning off Ripon Road he followed Swan Road past the Old Swan Hotel before turning and parking on Crescent Gardens. The old council offices were still vacant which always seemed so wasteful. *Probably will become more luxury apartments. Just what Harrogate needs!* he thought whilst taking the parking ticket from the machine. He slipped it on the dashboard before walking to a bench in the middle of the garden area. Even though the sun was shining the morning seemed cold. The Mercer Art Gallery would open shortly and he knew he would find peace and a degree of privacy there. He needed a place to think, to plan. Closing his eyes, he let the sun warm his face. He thought of the girl and he slipped her phone from his pocket. She was trapped within it, just like within her tube-like tomb, here in this small piece of technology she still existed. When the time and place was right – when it was safe – he would check her contacts. Switching on the phone might trigger an alert and the police would soon triangulate its location. That brief look would have to be carefully thought through. Patience was needed.

***

"Retrospective facial recognition technology." Harry let the words slip from his lips. Cyril stood behind him, a feeling of utter disdain at the idea. For one thing the word technology made him feel decidedly uncomfortable and the thought of using facial recognition went against what he believed the force stood for.

"The key word, sir, is retrospective. It's a tool. Think of it as a modern fingerprint technique or DNA collection. It's another weapon against the criminals. It allows us to identify unknowns from video or pictures. We can check Thompson's photographs against the custody records." He turned and grinned, a clear enthusiasm etched across his face. "The chance is we'll get zero results but we're trialling this and you never know. We could use it live alongside bodycams and linked with the town's CCTV but that's too *1984* for many. We have a responsibility to balance the human rights of the innocent with the rights of victims. When the missing and the dead cannot talk, we have this as a tool or, as some might say, and something I agree with, a weapon against the bad people."

"I am one of the many who believe it a step too far against human rights, Harry, but I do see your professional point." Cyril sat and folded his arms.

"It'll run the selected photographs in the background and we'll be notified of any positive identification of the faces within them. In the meantime, we're requesting help from people Sadie considered friends."

***

The gallery was warm and he was greeted with a smile from the lady near the entrance before exchanging a few words regarding the change in the weather. The room, although large, was separated by what could best be described as partitions set at ninety degrees to the walls on which were displayed the latest exhibition, a collection of abstract works that seemed not only chaotic and without real skill, but in total contrast to the elegance of the room in which they were displayed. Moving further inside he found the painting for which he was looking and stood, almost reverently, before it. He was immediately transported from day to night and to his past, a dark past that only moved into the light when he took control. He had first seen this painting when on a school visit and it had captivated him. It was entitled, *Silver Moonlight*. The skill and precision, the planning and the execution all contrived to encourage his enthusiasm for the artist, John Atkinson Grimshaw. He had no time to study and enjoy it for long as the phone in his pocket was of greater importance.

The bench, set at the same angle as the display walls, was neither inviting nor comfortable; it was possibly designed that way to prevent the public lingering too long. He needed to access Sadie's phone contacts, run through them alphabetically and inspect the images set within a circle as if under a microscope. He needed a location with no signal and no Internet.

***

"Bingo!" The word slipped from Harry's lips with great enthusiasm. "We have a hit."

Cyril leaned forward. In the background of a group photograph was a face highlighted within a white square alongside the photograph from the custody records. "What are the dots and lines?" Cyril pointed to the record.

"It's how the technology works; it highlights key facial features and then matches those with that one in the group shot. It's not one hundred percent but considering the quality of the phone photograph ..."

"Who is it?"

"Steven Speakman, drugs possession, GBH, theft. He's twenty-seven."

"Where was the photograph taken?"

"Logged on the phone's record as the pub on Cheltenham Parade and showing two weeks ago. Kindly gives a map."

"What did we do before smart phones, Harry?"

"You'll be saying that about facial recognition in a few years!"

"If you say so but I may well be a thing of the past by the time it becomes the norm." Cyril winked. "Owen can pay him a visit. Is he still local?"

Flicking through the file on screen he nodded. "We've still more to assess."

Cyril left and went to the Incident Room. Shakti was going through the notes delivered by Thompson detailing their mutual friends.

"I've run the names but so far there's nothing." She turned and he watched as her finger stabbed a name on the list. We received a call through the helpline number from this girl on the list. Rachel Gaunt, a school friend. Needs to talk about Sadie. She's due in thirty minutes. Her word 'needs' implied importance."

"Keep it informal and use the interview lounge, it's less intimidating. We've identified a Steven Speakman from the photographs. He's known to us for a number of offences. Progress, Shakti, progress."

***

Rachel Gaunt was early and the desk sergeant could clearly see she was nervous. Shakti was waiting and quickly escorted her to the lounge. The room was light and the furnishing less governmental but still the chairs were upholstered in blue and the walls displayed a collection of faded photographs of Harrogate. As they moved to sit an air freshener positioned on a window sill gasped bringing to the room a faint smell of lavender. However, the welcome was warm. Rachel refused the offer of coffee.

"I don't really know if I should be here never mind saying what I'm going to say knowing she's still missing. I'm aware the days are passing and the longer she's not found the more concerning it will be for all her family and friends." There was an extended pause.

"How well do you know Sadie?"

"Did. Knew her at school. We were never the closest of friends but we knew the same people and went to the same places. Look, I don't want this to sound like I'm bitching as I know the severity of the situation but people quickly gained the wrong impression of her. Firstly, she was beautiful and funny, a perfect body size and she surrounded herself with lots of people, particularly boys, but what she didn't have was any sense of kindness if that makes sense. She was spoiled. She could be bloody cruel. Some said she lacked a strong moral compass. What she wanted she would try to achieve irrespective of the feelings of others. What was strange is she never seemed to create enemies just drift away from people."

"You're twenty-one?" Shakti checked her notes.

"Yes, known her seven years but that's a guess. I knew her before then but only as another student."

"But you were friends, John Thompson listed you as such."

"Yes, that's why I know her still. She was never academic, but did enough. That's why she works where she does. Never had ambition other than to find the right man and believe me she certainly tried hard there. She's money driven, that's why she's still living at home. Her parents still treat her like a kid. Bought her a car only she's not passed her test. You knew that?"

"We knew she had the scooter until she could drive legally."

"She needed the freedom the bike offered. Didn't like her parents being part of her social life. She kept that private. Even John's unaware."

"Unaware?"

"He's not the only man. 'God made the flowers colourful and pretty to attract the insects', she often said. 'I follow the same theory and I must attract the best'. She had a dark side; she could be quite an unpleasant person."

"The others – the insects, did she say?"

Rachel nodded her head.

"Why are you here, Rachel?"

"Why am I here? What cliché shall I use? Don't judge a book by its cover. Our Sadie has a life that many didn't see. People cover for her, excuse her because she's beautiful and a good laugh."

"How has she hurt you?"

She laughed. "She knew I wanted John and we went out a few times, got on really well. She knew it and ... as the Dolly Parton song says, 'Don't take him 'cos you can'. But she did, she was seeing others too."

"So, I ask again why are you really here, Rachel?"

"In life we cast a shadow but for some there's more, according to my scientific understanding, it's known as a penumbra, something that can be important yet easily missed, an outer shadow. Families and loved ones often turn a blind eye because they see the things they don't want to see. Maybe they glimpse it briefly and they then question if what they saw was real. There could be someone out there whom she's truly pissed off in that moment. Shadows are only here when the sun shines and can soon vanish, we could say they're a bit like our dark moods and uncontrollable emotional outrages: periods of darkness in which we might act out of character or some might say, we show our true personality." She laughed, an embarrassed laugh that was shallow and without sincerity. "I don't know." She shrugged her shoulders. "What do I know? Maybe on the other hand, if she's just upped and gone, she's gone because someone can move her to the next level."

"How much has she pissed you off? Do you know where she is, Rachel?"

There was a pause. Rachel stared back directly at Shakti. There appeared to be a little anger in her tone. "If I knew I'd have told you from the outset. I came here out of concern. You and I know that people can project a different persona depending on who they're with. Although I don't like her, I also don't hate her and I wouldn't want something dreadful to happen to her. I came here to give you my opinion of the missing person, of Sadie, an opinion that might be of value to the investigation. That's what was requested by your lot from the general public. What you do with that information, that new knowledge I have given you is, I guess, now your choice." She stood. "But I have said it and that's important to me. Unless there's something else?"

"There is." She looked at her notes. "Do you know a Steven Speakman?"

"No, should I?" Rachel's answer was brusque.

Shakti remained expressionless. "There was always a possibility. I had to ask. Thank you for your time and co-operation." As the interview closed the atmosphere was now a lot less cordial.

Going back to the Incident Room, Shakti collected a felt pen and added the word *penumbra* onto a whiteboard followed by the meaning – a peripheral or indeterminate area or group. She wondered who might be on the periphery of Sadie's world. Rachel clearly believed there were a few.

Chapter Thirteen

Low Wath Road snaked from Pateley Bridge along the valley, narrow and undulating and constrained between drystone walls. The road was quiet as he approached Gouthwaite Reservoir; the stone lodge, a classic piece of Gothic architecture matched the intricate craftsmanship of the dam wall, its beauty now mostly hidden within trees. The road flanked the water's edge until reaching Ramsgill. He did not have far to drive before he would turn away from the road on entering Lofthouse. Stean was barely half a mile away.

He leaned on the car's roof. The afternoon was still clear and the clouds, the mares' tails, appeared so high, so ethereal. A faint halo-like spectrum was visible in a number of places as the sun shone through them creating what appeared to be tiny jewels. It seemed cold once outside, the car had been a cocoon of warmth. The valley breeze brought with it a shiver, even for July.

The single-track lane was signposted to the gorge and caution was the key as the road meandered and undulated guarded by tall walls and vegetation until reaching the turning for the site; the entrance was flanked by wood lap buildings and across the track was positioned a raised hump that brought the car to a crawl. His eyes scanned through one hundred and eighty degrees. Two parked motorcycles glinted in the sunshine. He paused and observed the car park set across the bridge that spanned the irregular crevice cut by nature that ran deep through the site. The bridge comprised wooden walkways to either side and centre leaving two tracks of metal grilles on which vehicles crossed. The rattle echoed down into the gulley as he passed.

The site was more haphazard than he had recalled. The car park was full, builders were constructing wooden lodges and temporary fencing had been erected constricting much of the area. For a moment there was a real concern as to whether he should be there but he only wanted to achieve one objective that would leave no visible or memorable trace. He locked the car and walked back over the bridge stopping only momentarily to stare into the open fissure at the tumbling water below.

The cafe within the visitors' centre was quiet.

"Not be a moment, love," the waitress busied past. "Menu's on the table."

Collecting one he moved towards the glazed wall to the far side of the room. Glass covered part of the floor too and he stared down into the gorge. His eyes tracked right and he saw the reason for his visit, Tom Taylor's Cave.

"What can I get you?"

He had not heard her approach and he was startled. She pointed to the menu.

"I get dizzy standing on that glass too. Always feel it's going to break." Her smile was welcoming.

He stepped away. "Bacon sandwich, well done, please."

"Butter, no butter or dipping?"

"Dipping?"

"We dip the bread into the pan, like fried slice. I have mine like that. Can you feel your arteries hardening as we speak?" She giggled.

"Then dipped would be just perfect. And tea. Thank you."

"Take a seat and it won't be long."

He thought of his own kitchen. 'Dipping, now there's an idea."

The Internet page for the site had clearly stated that there was no point bringing a mobile phone as there was definitely no signal but a public phone was available. 'How long is it since I used one of those? Like travelling back in time,' he thought. There needed to be no signal, that had to be the case as a mistake at this stage might alert the police that the phone was switched on.

She brought the food.

"Are you sure you can't get a phone signal here?" he asked holding up his own phone.

"No, love, unless you log on to our Internet."

"What about down in the gorge?"

She shook her head. "Nope and in the cave, Tom's cave, you are as communicative with the world as a Neanderthal! If you go over to that field, you can go in where they come out and see for yourself. Private call, is it?" She winked and chuckled at her own joke. "I'll get your tea."

Boots tied, he slipped on an additional sweater. He bought a ticket and received a plan and a hard hat. He checked his torch was working before setting off into the gorge. As double indemnity, he would wait until inside Tom

Taylor's Cave before switching on Sadie's phone, as there and below ground it would not reach a phone mast. The idea brought a smile as the cave was named after an apocryphal highwayman; like now, he would return here with his booty and he liked the idea. The water that had settled at the bottom of the passageway grew to be a ribbon of artificial light. The poem came into his head once again.

Pausing at what he believed to be the mid-point, he switched off the torch. The wet, cave sides now began to constrict his ability to move forward. The darkness was palpable. The sound of running water and distant voices seemed to echo within the chamber and yet there was an eerie peace. He thought of Sadie; raising his arms, he mimicked the position she was in when he slid her into the tube. "Imagine this being it, my final resting place, trapped forever in this highwayman's lair."

On approaching the sloping cave exit that climbed into the field, he stopped, resting against the stone side. A circle of light was now above him, steps in the ground climbed upwards to what was a stone wall. "It's like being born," he whispered as he took out his own phone. There was no signal. It was now or never. He would not find a more secure location without Internet or phone signals. Two visitors squeezed past and politely made comments, one thankful she was leaving the cave.

"Never felt so claustrophobic," she giggled but there was clearly relief in her voice. "Trousers and bloody shoes are soaking too. A romantic weekend in The Dales, you said it would be! Romantic? It will now cost you wine and the biggest slice of cake they sell. You promised that when I was paralysed with fear in there!" She slapped her partner on the back. They continued to laugh as they perched on a rounded rock a little further out at the cave's mouth. She removed her phone and they took some selfie photographs.

Pressing the button on the top of Sadie's phone, the apple appeared illuminated white on the black screen, before the request for a password appeared. He tapped in the numbers he had put in after changing her security number. He had used her fingerprint when she was in the car and changed the password before sending the spurious texts based on her contacts and frequent messages, carefully keeping the transmission within the area in which she would have been expected to be. The call and text to her boyfriend had been a careless error.

"Excuse me, sorry to bother you but could you please take a photograph of us?"

Startled, he turned to see the girl had recovered from her ordeal and was proffering her phone. He fumbled with Sadie's phone slipping it up his sleeve and added a false smile. "You need evidence of the trauma to which you have been subjected I take it? We men are all the same."

She laughed. If only she knew.

"There you go. One more just to make sure. Hope you feel better in the sunshine."

"Too right I will." She leaned down to retrieve her phone and laughter erupted again.

"Enjoy the wine!"

"Oh! I most certainly will."

They took a few more pictures and then moved away up and out of the tree-lined hollow and through the gap in the surrounding wall.

Retrieving Sadie's phone, he located the contact folder.

Scanning down, he stopped at female names and then only those showing an image within the circle. Some had no image just initials. They were of no interest. He stopped at one specific contact that caught his eye. *There's a name of the nineties!* The thought was immediate. "Jessica," the name was said quietly whilst extending the last vowel. "Let's discover more." The *Top Gear* tune flooded his mind whilst scrolling down the entry of Jessica's contact details – email, phone and conveniently her address alongside a map locating the house. He photographed the details using the camera on his phone before finding two more, they would be reserves if Jessica proved to be unsuitable, "You just never know when opportunities appear." He switched off the phone. More people began to emerge from the cave, their echoing voices growing ever closer.

Within the hour Sadie's phone was thrown into Gouthwaite Reservoir, to sink into the mud and be lost, a fate that just might befall Jessica in the not-too-distant future. Patience, however, would be the key. He had made that his mantra having committed one serious error already.

***

Owen pulled the car into the kerb and scanned the numbers on the doors. "Number thirteen. Lucky bugger!" he mumbled as he turned to look at Brian. The records showed Steven Speakman was unemployed and receiving benefits. The curtains in the lower window moved after they had opened the gate. A dog started to bark from within the house. Owen stood back as Brian went to the door. It opened as he raised his hand to knock.

"Members of our wonderful constabulary if I'm not mistaken." Speakman was dressed in a loose grey fleece tracksuit, the Under Armour label visible. He rested a hand on the door frame, clearly sending a signal suggesting the way was barred. Brian noted that he was pumped, his biceps bulged in his sleeves. He was not fazed. Steroids did this to young men, a kind of deformity. He looked at Speakman's head, it was shaved out of necessity owing to clear signs of premature balding. The drugs did that too.

"Your wonderful constabulary politely request five minutes of your valuable time, Mr Speakman." Brian put his hand on the opposite side of the door frame mimicking two Toby jugs. Owen stood by the gate.

"I'll have to consult my diary but I think my next few dances are fully booked." The grin showed a missing front tooth and staining to most of the others.

"Now that's a real shame as we'll have to bring friends and continue this tête-à-tête at the station. It's up to you if you can squeeze in a quick waltz or foxtrot."

Speakman lowered his arm. "I'll need a minute to sort the dog."

Owen entered first. The room, although small, was tidy. A large dog bed placed in one corner accounted for the slight aroma in the room.

"I'm clean and I've done nothing."

Brian stared at the tattoo running up his neck.

Owen slipped the photograph over but said nothing. He watched as Speakman's face wrinkled. "Remember that?"

"I do. We were either in the ..." he paused. "No, Cheltenham Inn. There was a party on and we just joined in. There was no trouble, if I remember correctly."

"Do you know the girl in the picture?" Brian asked.

"Not personally but I know she was, let's just say,

having a good time as were her friends." He put the back of his hand to his nose and sniffed. "All girls in the group if I recall." He handed the photograph back. "Didn't know I was being photographed but then how could pretty girls resist?" He chuckled. "Any more pics?"

"Cocaine?" Owen asked popping the photograph into his pocket.

"Certainly not Beecham's Powder. What do you boys always say ... allegedly."

"And you didn't know her?"

"Nope. Who is she anyway?" Speakman took a roll-up from a tin and lit it. After inhaling he quickly picked a piece of tobacco from the tip of his tongue.

"Sadie Vance. Gone missing. Not heard or seen of for some time. She's nineteen."

Speakman exhaled a smoke ring and watched it slowly disappear. "In with a bad crowd? Not paid certain debts maybe? Age and sex will mean nothing to some of the bastards who are out there shifting the stuff. Sorry, but I was just there on the night and it's coincidental that I was in the photograph. There are others but only my face. We just had a laugh. Besides, that party was a while ago. Weeks! She been missing since then?"

Brian shook his head. "No, only days. Who did you go there with?"

"Ant Clark and Gary Barton. You can see the back of Ant's head on your photograph. Getting to look more like a monk by the week. Dead conscious of the patch he is. I told him to shave the bloody lot off!"

"Gary was at the bar?" Brian did not try to hide his cynicism.

"It'd be a bloody first if he was. More likely having a piss if it was time to get a round in."

The answer brought a smile. "If you hear anything …" Brian did not finish the sentence but stood. The dog started barking in the next room as they moved to the door. "Dangerous dog?"

Speakman went to the door at the far end of the room and opened it. A black cocker spaniel shot out and ran immediately towards Owen who was still sitting before leaping onto his knee, all wagging tail and lolling tongue. In its excitement it peed on his trousers. Owen pushed the dog away and stood.

"Meet Chester … a real danger! Sorry, incontinent when excited and he's got dreadful breath!" Speakman could not fail to keep the smile from his face.

Brian laughed as Owen extricated himself from the dog.

"Sorry about that. He's my girlfriend's but she's at work."

Owen looked at the urine dribbling onto his shoe.

Speakman took hold of Chester's collar and put him back into the other room.

"One question. How on earth did you link me to that photograph?"

Neither officer answered the question but Owen nodded. "As I said, thanks for your co-operation. Can't say I love your dog!"

Sitting in the car Brian handed Owen a box of tissues.

"Not what I was expecting, Brian. Bright lad that, not your usual. He knows nothing but his observations about the drugs have been logged. 'Dangerous dog?'" Owen mimicked Brian's question. "Too bloody right, Smirthwaite, Killer breath and … look at my kecks and shoes." He continued to dab them with the tissue.

"Sorry! The bark sounded as if it came from something larger."

"I'd have been bloody drowned if it had been! Just drive."

Back at the station Owen added the two names of Clark and Barton into the system. Neither came back positive.

Chapter 14

The day had dawned early. The blackbird ate sultanas from the home-made bird table positioned on the small wall to the edge of the garden. The coffee mug cupped in his hands released a rich aroma. The early light had made sleeping difficult but there was also a sense of excitement; the chase was often the best part bringing butterflies and a degree of nausea, not unpleasant, a bit like the feeling before taking a theme park ride. It was like testing oneself against the unknown – a fear and anxiety that was controlled risk. *The doubters thought I couldn't take them.* The room was quiet, even Lord Byron was still. Concentrating, he could make out the tick of the clock on the windowsill. It was steady, a heartbeat.

The three names retrieved from Sadie's phone were neatly written on the notepad. Name and contact details including social media addresses were added. "The social media handle!" he said to himself as he opened Facebook on the laptop. "Let's see what Jessica's world is really like."

The cover photograph was a collection of young women dressed for a night out, each held a certain pose as well as a Champagne flute. Sadie was the third from the left. Jessica was centre stage with a glass in each hand. Only one of the other girls he had retrieved from the phone he identified as present.

Jessica's profile image was another selfie, all pouting lips and seductive eyes. It surprised him when considering her profession. The general info and bio then drew his attention. She was perfect. Working with teeth and with a surname of *White* seemed to him to be fate. She was twenty-two.

Dental Assistant
Wellington Grove High
Woodhouse Primary School

He checked her photographs and collated the information needed to build a better picture of her. It would be a critical assessment allowing the formulation of the plan. For the moment, at least, there was no need to investigate the other names on the list. Jessica White was just perfect.

Narrowing his eyes, he focused on the cover photograph weighing Jessica's physical stature against that of Sadie. If anything, she was shorter but probably the same body size. He knew he could ill afford anyone with a fuller figure. Sitting back, he steepled his fingers. A frantic scratching from the cage on the end of the work surface brought a distraction.

"You're awake, Lord Byron! How good of you to join me."

Taking the laptop across to the hamster cage he turned the screen. "I do hope we'll soon have another friend to join us. Just one more and then it's back to normality: this extended intrusion will soon come to a close. You can have too many new friends. I know this from the past, you can promise too much to too many. People will get upset and then they can spoil things. Two and maybe, just maybe, we can think of more in the future but who knows what will happen if our old friends appear in the news."

Closing the laptop, he concentrated on Jessica's address. Unlike Sadie, she appeared to live in an apartment. Did she live alone? It was of little consequence and besides he was not planning on going inside. She would come to him. That's how it worked. People always came if you were patient. He checked the time, he would leave in an hour.

Parking the car on Hollins Mews he would walk to Chatsworth Grove. From Coppice Drive he turned onto Luchon Way, a cycle and pedestrian route that linked the area to the town's centre. He read the sign to the right of the path. Luchon Way was named after Bagneres-de-Luchon, Harrogate's twin town in the French Pyrenees and a regular part of the Tour de France route. He mimicked Michael Caine, "Not a lot of people know that!" He chuckled to himself and walked down the narrow, Tarmacked pathway. Two cyclists approached and he stood to one side and was greeted with a wave and thanks. The pathway sat in a natural valley and trees and shrubs bordered the outer edges before giving way to manicured grass. Considering the proximity to buildings there was a natural ambience enhanced by the constant bird song. Looking to his right were a number of apartment blocks, one of which he knew would be Jessica's. Today he would locate it and this step was all part of the planning process, each step was vital and a critical part of the excitement. *Like foreplay, nothing should be rushed,* he thought and it brought a smile to his lips.

***

The Westminster Arcade seemed warm but deplete of shops. The black and white floor tiles gave the Victorian building an air of sophistication but it seemed hollow and full of echoes. Since the closure of Cordings' Country Clothing shop, the entrance seemed to be less welcoming. Soon the bookshop would go too. He had been looking forward to lunch and his stomach had reminded him of the approaching appointment for too long. Mounting the stairs to the second floor Owen knew Cyril would already be there, he was always punctual if not early. He was correct and noticed Cyril look up and then glance at his watch.

"Am I late, sir?" Owen checked his own watch and gave his wrist a shake. "Looks okay but I was given this watch recently and it seems to be missing its previous owner!"

Cyril laughed. "On time. Lunch and I bet you're ready."

"Too right I am."

Tony, the owner, waved and came to the table. "Lovely to see you, Owen, seems a while. The baby distracting you?"

Owen almost dribbled the next few sentences giving a full explanation of the progress the sprog was making.

"It's Christopher, not 'sprog' I believe?" Tony looked at Cyril for confirmation with one eyebrow raised.

Cyril chuckled. "He'll talk about the wonders of parenthood for hours if you give him the opportunity. Suffice it to say, all is well. I've ordered, Owen. Your turn otherwise the day will be gone."

"Sorry, get a little carried away. Funny how something so small can have such a huge influence on all aspects of my life. Whatever he's having but a bit more if you get my drift."

"He's eating for two, Tony. Cheese on toast with an extra round!"

"And a latte, please."

"This arcade gets emptier every time we come." Owen squeezed his legs under the table. "Thank goodness for the Harrogate Tea Room. We were chatting this morning, April and a few others. We never found the girl who went missing in Knaresborough and the longer this goes on the more I feel we're looking at a similar ..."

Cyril's look brought a stop to the sentence. "Murder? Is that what you thought?" He pulled the kind of face that suggested he was not convinced. "If my memory serves me well, that person neither had a smart phone nor was she linked to any social media sites unlike this case. That made things far more difficult. It was very hard to just vanish even then, but today with the technology that's all around us it's nigh on impossible. How many cameras have you been on just getting here?"

"A shed load, but it's been five days, sir. Five days with all the technology we have at our fingertips."

"And it was five weeks before a murder enquiry was launched with the case you mentioned."

"The evidence we have is nebulous. It's stalled." Owen placed his elbows on the table and put his chin on his hands.

Cyril raised an eyebrow. Owen's vocabulary was certainly improving. "Nebulous?" He said the word slowly. "Interesting."

The food arrived. It had not been on the table long before Owen's tie rested within the melted cheese.

"Your tie, Owen, is eating your lunch."

Owen swiftly collected it and slipped it into his mouth removing any food that had collected.

"Quelle finesse, my friend, quelle finesse," Cyril whispered under his breath.

"Sir?"

"We'd never swop you!"

Nothing more was said until they had finished their meal.

"I have a bad feeling, sir." He stuck a finger into his mouth working a nail between two back teeth. "Have I got a pepper corn or something stuck here?"

Cyril gave a brief glance at the offered open mouth and shook his head. He could not abide bodily fluids and the thought of staring into Owen's mouth so soon after the mastication of food brought a certain revulsion.

Owen continued. "In all the missing person cases I've witnessed, most times there was an innocent explanation, human frailty like, but they turned up, usually red faced and embarrassed by the fuss and upset they'd caused or they were found hanging in some remote spot or a garage. Some even decide to rearrange the front of a train. Mind, others are just as angry to have been found at all. One, I recall, was enjoying a second life with his lover and her two kids and neither family was aware of the other's existence. There was no remorse either on his behalf just anger at being discovered."

"So, what's your theory, Owen?"

"Taken. She's been taken. Opportune and not fully planned is my initial guess. Well, I mean the kidnap was planned but she was not the specific target, any female would have done. It was a case of right place and time or wrong place … Hence the diversion that night. Had it not been there she might not have gone the way she did and …"

"Yes, yes. In your theoretical world is she now alive or dead as we sit here?"

Owen pulled his usual thinker's expression. "Dead and I'll tell you why." He sipped some coffee. "Keeping someone, especially a young woman, a woman with an illness that needs medication is a burden, a burden the kidnapper didn't anticipate. From Tom Ward's account, you know, the guy in the cafe who helped when the chap gave her grief. Well, he said she was feisty and wanted to give the bloke a slap. She might be small and cute but I believe she can be a bit of a spitfire. I get that impression from her boyfriend too. Then there are the anomalies as Carruthers keeps pointing out. Neither her parents nor the boyfriend seemed to know what she was up to. Some of her friends have said she could be, let's say, flirty. An eye for the men. Then we have Speakman's statement– the possible drugs. Doesn't tie up. The girl's parents think she is an angel but there could be a shadow lurking that none can see. She's lied too about the reason for her absence."

Cyril immediately reflected on the word *penumbra* he had seen written on the board in the Incident Room but said nothing.

"You tracked her phone history and tied the loose ends and there was nothing until she went missing." Cyril waved his hand and made a writing gesture aimed at Tony, requesting the bill.

"People can have two phones and the second phone

might not be registered to them, so although we've done the search, we have nothing."

Cyril paid. Carrie popped her head from the kitchen and waved.

"Testicles, spectacles, wallet and watch." Cyril tapped his jacket checking he had collected everything from the table. "Keep me informed, Owen. See you tomorrow. Afternoon to myself," he grinned. "Appointment with a Black Sheep and then dinner out with the memsahib."

"If she heard you say that, you'd have one fewer item to check, probably two actually come to think of it!"

A supercilious grin spread over Cyril's face. "Maybe, Owen. I'll take the opportunity to pop my head in the Mobile Incident Unit."

On Owen's drive towards the police station a number of emergency vehicles were heading into Harrogate. Lights flashed and sirens screamed. On arrival he was met with news that a vehicle had collided with pedestrians.

***

Cyril sat quietly in the corner of the bar, his beer on the table. He jotted down notes from the lunchtime conversation. The more he scribbled the more he was coming round to believing Owen might well be correct in his interpretation of the evidence but if so, why no body? If it were deliberate, an argument or fallout there would be evidence. Unplanned murders were messy and careless. He underlined the word *planned*. The sound of sirens grew louder. His phone rang.

"Bennett."

"Major incident at the side door to the railway station. A car's failed to stop, mounted the pavement and hit a number of pedestrians. It might be terrorist motivated. The driver's done a runner." Owen sounded calm. "Thought if you were close."

"There's usually a police van at that location." Cyril did not wait for the answer, he was already on his way. The remains of the pint had been downed in one.

The scene was as expected. Blue lights illuminated buildings and reflected in the many windows. The one-way traffic continued along Station Parade albeit at a reduced speed and an officer tried desperately to keep the flow moving. The drivers, rubbernecking to see what was happening, brought the traffic to almost a standstill. The pavement on the station side of the road was closed; the blue and white tape had been speedily stretched between any vertical object. Two ambulances stood waiting to take the injured to hospital. Like all such incidents a crowd had formed wherever there was a vantage point. Cyril crossed the road, ducked beneath the police tape and held his ID to the quickly advancing officer.

"Terrorism?" Cyril only offered the one word.

The officer turned to see if anyone was eavesdropping and then leaned forwards. "No, stolen car. It had been picked up on ANPR just before the incident. One of ours was in pursuit. The driver, a youth according to witnesses, buggered off down the pedestrian area. We have a description and he should soon be apprehended. A couple of injured needing hospital treatment but thankfully nobody was killed."

Cyril could see a paramedic attending one prostrate figure and one other of the injured being brought to the rear of the ambulance, a foil blanket around his shoulders. He turned to leave. There was nothing he could do. "Thanks." He nodded to the officer before ducking below the tape. He checked the road, crossed and headed for Robert Street.

Chapter 15

One footpath leading through the grounds of The Majestic Hotel ran towards the old gatehouse, a detached building set just before The Queen's Hall. The pathway, graced by grass to either side, was set some way from the hedges and trees bordering the pavement to the side of the A61. If positioned correctly he could stand and be away from any pedestrians and yet in full view of the building that sat across the road. Removing the small monocular from his pocket, he closed one eye as he looked at the building whilst allowing his fingers to rotate the focusing ring until the image sharpened. Scanning the building's façade he paused at the door, a double set of steps flanked by black wrought iron railings led away from the portal. He positioned a finger over the front lens and all went black and then moved it away. According to her Facebook page this was Jessica's place of work. He brought the monocular away from his face and was about to slip it into his pocket when the door opened. He paused. Removing a tissue, he rubbed the lens whilst he watched. A woman exited leaving the door ajar. She stood momentarily on the upper level. A flush of excitement caused him to turn and check behind, he was still alone. Bringing the monocular towards his eye he stared at the woman.

Malcolm Hollingdrake

Jessica White rubbed the back of her neck and breathed a deep sigh as the fresh air filled her lungs. She could now pause and take a moment before grabbing a coffee and a late lunch, it had been a busy morning. She quickly looked at her mobile but had little enthusiasm and put it back into her pocket. Before her was the dental practice car park, once the front garden of the large Victorian house. It had been her place of work for nearly two years, and often the spot for a moment's respite away from the clean, clinical smell of the surgery. The area had been strategically planned to create the maximum number of parking places whilst retaining some shrubbery, part of which was a low privet hedge running before the pavement edge. She concentrated on the sound of what appeared to be an orchestra of sirens way off towards the centre of town. They brought a shiver to her neck as she immediately thought of Sadie. "Where the bloody hell are you, girl?" Her words, almost a whisper, were lost as if carried on the slight breeze that moved her hair like rushes in a stream. Wrapping her arms across her chest she stared at the sky. The clouds moved as lethargically as she felt. The song of a bird drew her attention, its greenish plumage as colourful as its rattling, shrill song.

From across the road, a false eye was clearly focused on her. Camouflaged by the foliage the observer weighed up the young woman, confirming height and weight as he had judged and contrasted the image from her Facebook picture. Her white scrubs, now partially hidden from view, were in marked contrast to the dark grey of the practice's stone façade. To his amazement he had seen her come out, watched her look in the direction of the town and now

103

she looked at the sky. He did not move but felt the same flutter of excitement he had experienced on seeing Sadie's forlorn figure. He saw the same innocence, the immediate vulnerability. He liked that. "To take you now, to snatch you. Your colleagues would wonder where you'd gone." He chuckled and shook his head. "Alas my dear, not there, not now. I see the cameras positioned on the car park. Maybe, just maybe they can see me. I stare at you and the cameras stare back, but they look blindly without thought or real purpose." Lifting the monocular he scanned the windows. In the upper window a face stared out, direct, the expression showing uncertainty. *Could I be seen?* His thoughts were rapid and fearful. He looked again but now the person was gone, only for them to appear at the door. The gesture told him everything, the pointing finger, the speed at which the stairs were taken. His face flushed and the excitement was quickly replaced by the flutter of fear. Slipping the monocular into his pocket he moved away until concealed by the thicker vegetation. A further move would take him out towards the rear of the hotel. A group of people moved in his direction and he quickly walked behind them.

Jessica responded to the call. A hand touched her shoulder.

"Are you alright? Did you see him?" Connie Ashcroft was breathless, her anxiety clear to see.

Jessica's facial expression answered the question. "The beautiful bird?"

"No! Over there, maybe he was hidden to you but from up there, from the window, I could see him looking this way. I think he had a telescope."

"There was a bird, beautiful – there, in the tree, it's still there. Look!" she pointed in the direction. "Maybe he too had seen it."

Her colleague looked in the direction and saw it before turning to look across the road. The man had gone.

"Come on, coffee and a sandwich are much needed before this afternoon's onslaught," Jessica cajoled before linking arms with her colleague and offering a reassuring smile. Connie raised herself on tiptoe still hoping to see the man, to prove the reason for her concern was real but he had disappeared.

The two mounted the steps but only one looked back into the hotel grounds uncertain now as to what she had seen.

***

Owen took little interest in the hit and run as initial supposition of a terrorist threat had quickly evaporated after the youth had been apprehended near the town's library. He was known to them – driving ban, no insurance and under the influence of both drugs and alcohol.

"A case for locking the door and tossing the key away. They never learn," Owen grumbled as he slipped the lanyard round his neck. "Waste more time with these buggers than we should. Lock him up!"

On reaching his desk he fumbled in the mug for an Uncle Joe's mint and found one first time. He felt his shoulders relax. *It's the little things in life*, he thought.

***

"The guy I saw, do you think we should report it?" Connie removed the empty coffee mug from the table in front of Jessica.

There was a pause. "For what?"

"Voyeurism? The fact that one of your best mates has disappeared and there's some pervert watching you with a spyglass."

"Spyglass, bloody hell, there's a word from the dark and distant past – perverts and pirates are alive and well and living in Harrogate." Jessica's smile was genuine. "So, you believe this pervert positioned himself knowing I was going to go out onto the car park. I didn't even know I was going out until two minutes before I did. It was the bird he was watching, not me. Ornithologists, Twits, I think they call themselves, always carry binoculars, or spyglasses. They're always watching, ready and patient to be alerted about the rare and unusual birds. I believe they have a linked phone system where they contact each other and then once one spots something rare, they all come flocking! Sorry for the pun. I've seen them watching the kite hovering over town with their spyglasses. Even I stop and look at it when I spot it. Speaking of patient, we've jobs to do." She looked at the clock on the wall.

The afternoon passed more quickly than she could have hoped. Jessica was relieved when the last patient left. After another forty minutes cleaning and prep, she would be gone too. On leaving she stood on the top step and looked across at the hotel garden. A child's laughter somewhere hidden behind the hedge brought a smile. Looking at the tree she recalled the bird. *The world would be a sadder place without our feathered friends*, she thought. It would take her fifteen minutes to walk home. However, there was a nag, a worry as she paused by the entrance to the car park. The road was busy. She had decided at lunch time to stick to the road, she would not take Luchon Way, even though it was sunny and bright; the children would be playing in the playground area. "Just this once I'll play safe," she reassuringly said to herself, "otherwise you'll grow afraid of your bloody own shadow!"

Once home, she tossed her bag onto the settee and moved to the window. Three children were playing hopscotch in the open area by the line of garages. Folding her arms, she shook her head as memories came flooding back. *How long is it since I ...* Her thoughts were interrupted by her mobile's ring tone. It was Connie Ashcroft.

"Maybe you were right and I was wrong. I've just looked at the Harrogate web page and you'll never believe it but there's news of a sighting of a rare bird, a Eurasian Siskin. It was seen near the Conference Centre and other parts of town during most of the day and it's attracted a number of watchers. There are even some photographs."

"I looked them up, the birdwatchers, that is, they're called Twitchers not Twits and certainly not as you thought, perverts!" They both chuckled. "I took your advice and stayed on the roads."

"I've tagged you onto the site. See if it's the bird you saw. You out tonight?"

"I may walk into town for a gin or two but now it's a shower and food. Thanks for your concern today, hun."

"Have one for me. Another word from the wise, don't have kids, your freedom evaporates faster than ether!"

Jessica giggled. "You've been working with a dentist for far too long."

***

Owen lay on his back on the settee and held his son above

him on stretched arms. The raspberry sound produced from his pursed lips in an attempt to emulate the noise of a speeding aircraft, brought a giggle and a dribble from Christopher. "Superman," Owen continued to make the sound and the giggles grew louder.

"Father and son in perfect harmony!" Hannah popped her head around the door. "He'll throw up if you jiggle him around much more." The giggles continued briefly. The words had barely left her lips when a stream of white liquid headed directly at Owen's face.

"You always seem to attract it, if it's not on your tie it's on your suit. Pass him here and go and clean up. I'll pop him in his cot. Tea in ten." She moved over and took the child before kissing Owen's hand. "That's the only part of you not contaminated."

For a big man he had the expression of total innocence. He licked his white lips. "Tonight's starter is a tad sweet."

"Behave!"

Christopher settled quickly and Owen sipped a beer. "Do you miss not having alcohol?"

"No, I have maternal responsibilities and a boss who has advised what's best for our son. And what Dr Julie Pritchett says goes – just as she guides Cyril!"

Owen held up his beer glass. "I don't think I could give birth as I couldn't give up beer for a year."

"You couldn't give birth even if a large star appeared in the east! You are, the last time I looked at least, a man and contrary to what some folks think these days no matter how many times we have sex you'll not become pregnant, you're safe to keep on drinking. Any news on the girl?"

"No and that is never good. It's been too long." He

looked at Christopher. "Imagine how her parents must feel, total impotence and we're not helping. Drawn a blank on everything. Phone, CCTV, friends, cranks and potential positive IDs from the public have all gone through the sieve, but nothing. The vagaries are what we have and they worry me. The texts, the secrets. If your loved ones were kept in the shadows how the hell are we supposed to discover the truth?"

"You think she's dead, I can tell."

"Probably soon after she was taken. I don't know why other than what I've just said. I've read the files on a number of missing persons and this one doesn't follow the pattern."

Hannah slipped her hand across the table and placed it on his as she glanced at the child now asleep to her left. "I do hope that you're wrong."

Owen just nodded and squeezed her hand.

Chapter 16

It was worth the wait. The dashboard clock showed just before eight. The sky was still milky blue but to the east it was darkening as the western sky grew into richer and warmer hues. Jessica moved away from the building towards the line of garages, a matching row of five. She paused as her eyes were drawn to the chalked numbered squares on the Tarmac. Looking round with a mixture of uncertainty and devilment she stood before the square marked with the number one. Placing her bag on the floor she hopped towards the top, turned and hopped back. A huge grin spread across her face as she thrust a clenched fist into the air. *Like riding a bike, you never forget.* Collecting the bag, she moved off heading for the main road.

The same eyes watched from the security of the car, the same eyes that had watched her at lunchtime. There was now a greater eagerness to come face to face. It did not take much to anticipate the direction in which she was heading. Within seconds the car had passed her as she walked towards town. Parking near the now-empty council offices he waited. Within ten minutes she was walking past her place of work, a minute later the exhibition hall.

Glancing at the sign he confirmed the parking was free after 6pm. Setting the car's alarm his first destination was the junction of Crescent Road and Parliament Street. He jogged to the centre of the road before leaning on the railing that defended the central island before pressing the pelican crossing button. He was instructed to wait. On the opposite side of the junction, she crossed. A light skip came quickly into her step, the same agile movement he had just seen as she had danced over the chalk squares. Scanning the roads to her right, she quickened her pace. It was then she saw him, looked directly towards his position but she did not notice him, he was just another evening pedestrian, one of many – for her it was an inconsequential moment, for him they were face to face.

Leaving the sanctuary of the island he was soon close, close enough to reach out and touch her if he had wanted, close enough to smell the perfume that drifted and lingered in her wake. She turned into The Winter Gardens. The entrance was unusual, historical retaining much of its originality. Steps flowed both left and right descending to the cavernous bar area below. He cautiously followed lifting the hood on his jacket but not pausing, knowing cameras would be trained on the entry. He deliberately lowered his face just enough so he could still see her; she took the steps to the left. Looking from the upper level he stared down on the busy area, the bar running the full length to the left. The arched, glazed ceiling displayed the light of the dying day, now more yellow than blue; lights illuminated the alcoves and the lower level. That same void echoed to the many chattering voices, a drone that drowned the inconsequential piped music. He did not follow her, only his eyes tracked her progress towards the bar. He would wait a while, sit and observe. He screwed up his hand, his fingers making a cylinder and placed it to his eye, the majority of the scene now redacted, making Jessica the very centre of his attention.

"Can I get you something?"

The voice from behind brought a gasp and he twitched. He had neither seen nor heard the waiter approach. He swiftly removed his hand from his face. "No, no. Just looking for a friend." It was the first thing that came to mind. "I'll wait outside. They probably haven't arrived yet." He checked his watch. "I'm very early."

The waiter showed little interest, tucked the tray under his arm and descended the stairs at some pace.

Unnerved, he now needed to leave, wait back at the car. There was no plan, there never was or ever had been. If it were meant to be then she would be coming home with him and if not, there would be another time and place.

Arriving back at the car he removed the carboard tube he had saved from a roll of cling film; it was firm and stout, similar to the one he had used on Sadie. He let his fingers roll round the steering wheel. Time dragged like a lengthening shadow. There was no point watching the dashboard clock. He really needed to keep his eyes on one point in the distance, a point she had passed when coming into town. It was so easy to be distracted, to focus on the wrong people. That was not the way, he had to concentrate. His body relaxed. The pleasure after all was not in the having but in the attaining. Letting his fingers drum on the passenger seat, a slow rhythm, like counting the seconds, brought Sadie to mind and he remembered her face, her distress. It brought neither pleasure nor remorse. He checked the clock again. It was 10.15.

***

April Richmond ran with Ralph, her Great Dane, along the edge of The Stray. Myriad coloured lights festooned the roadside trees bringing a certain magic. When out with him in the late evening she kept him on the leash. The dog tolerated her pace, his movement was neither a run nor a walk, it was more a lope. It was good to be out, to clear her head. She had given her support to colleagues dealing with the earlier hit and run, concluded some cases that were going to court and looked in on the investigation of the missing girl, Sadie Vance. She had stared at the boards and the girl's photograph and like Owen, she felt uncomfortable with the lack of progress. The writing was on the wall, the evidence, but no one could decipher it. She remembered the word penumbra. "Hiding in the shadow of a shadow," she whispered to herself. Nothing if not determined, she decided then that she would research similar cases but tie it within a narrow time scale. A national search might throw up similarities. She slowed her pace until she came to a standstill allowing her hands to drop to her knees and she breathed deeply. She had had enough of this day.

***

"Everything comes to those who wait." The words slipped from his lips as he raised himself in the seat. One hand reached for the key whilst the other touched the card tube. The engine started but the car remained stationary. She was not alone. The couple, both female, had crossed Crescent Road together and they paused deep in conversation. Would they walk the same way? That was out of his control. If they did, he would pull away and go home but if not ...

"Are you okay on your own, we could share a cab?" Jessica's request was expressed more for herself than the friend.

"No, you know it's only by the park and it's not late. See, there's still some light in the sky!"

Jessica frowned. "You get more light from a bloody candle. I'll walk with you it's ..." she did not finish the sentence.

"'I'll walk with you'?" she repeated Jessica's offer. "Are you nervous? Is it the thought of Sadie? You know her, she was always a silly little cow. She's disappeared to make a point, probably not got her own way. You know how hot-headed she can be. Liar and schemer when she was at school, at least. Went with a boyfriend of mine and told me to my face that she hadn't but he told me she offered it on a plate."

"I'm fine. If I start to worry then I'll do nothing on my own. Thanks for a great night. Just what I needed and I'll keep my eyes open for them Twitchers!"

They laughed, hugged and went their separate ways. To the watcher in the car his stomach fluttered with the anticipation. He watched them kiss, wave and move apart.

Ripon Road had been busy and her initial anxiety had dissipated. She was nearly home and a feeling of foolishness began to weigh heavily. She did not know whether to laugh or cry. She walked up the shallow incline from Hampsthwaite Road towards her apartment block, her eyes finding the chalked hopscotch squares in the dim light.

eyes finding the chalked hopscotch squares in the dim light. She did not see the car nor the person standing by it.

"Miss White?" The voice was soft and non-threatening.

Jessica turned and she saw the figure approaching from only a couple of metres away. The proximity startled her. She felt her stomach churn and her legs weaken. "Who are ..." she did not finish the sentence.

"Did you enjoy your hopscotch. You were very good." There was sincerity in the words.

Momentarily she turned to look at the chalk squares, it was only for a second but that was time enough. The cardboard tube was already arcing to the side of her head and struck perfectly on her right side just below and behind her ear. She heard nothing else. She neither felt being caught nor carried the few metres to the car.

Chapter Seventeen

Owen woke to the sound of the baby crying. He reached across the bed but Hannah was not there, the sheets were cold. Hannah was in the lounge with Christopher in her arms, the crying now much louder.

He's been like this on and off all night." She held out the child. "I need the loo and ten minutes."

Owen put Christopher over his shoulder and bobbed up and down humming to the child. The crying stopped. He took him through to the bedroom and placed him gently in the crib at the foot of their bed before heading to the kitchen. He threw teabags into cups and flicked on the kettle. Hannah entered.

"As if by magic he stops. I haven't had a full hour's sleep and I didn't want him disturbing you. Now I face a day of the same. What do they say? It will pass, it's a phase." She sighed.

"Go to bed, I'll bring you tea." Owen leaned down and kissed her forehead. "I love you and I know just how much you are putting in."

Even before Owen arrived at the station, he knew the day was going to start badly. Every traffic light had been against him and the endless road works along Otley Road, created to construct new cycle lanes within the busy highway, exacerbated the situation. His slamming of the car door summed up his mood. The greeting from the desk officer confirmed his premonition.

"Morning, sadly not the best start to the day." He paused as he interpreted the full gamut of Owen's body language and expression. He turned, collected Owen's security lanyard and held it like some peace offering.

Owen paused and lowered his head briefly. "I note that you failed to use the word *good* before the word *morning* in your greeting. Pray tell why?"

"We may have another young woman missing. DC Chris Geldart is waiting to hand over."

Owen frowned, the name Chris made him think of Hannah and he flushed with guilt. He retrieved his ID lanyard and pass. "May? She's either missing or she's not." His tone was sharp and he raised his hand in a gesture of apology. "Sorry, bad morning so far."

Chris Geldart was waiting in the Incident Room. Even though he was nursing a coffee, Owen could see he had the expression of a tired man, a man who was eager for home and sleep after what appeared to have been a busy night. There was a relieved look on his face on seeing Owen.

"Apparently she was out with this person last night who sensed," Richard paused to look at the note he had made on the board, "Jessica White, the missing one, was extremely anxious. It's interesting to know that Jessica was also a friend of the other missing girl, Sadie Vance. This friend rang her to check she was alright this morning but received no answer so she went to her flat. She wasn't in. A neighbour told her she'd heard something about 11.15 but couldn't see anything when she looked outside. She also told her she'd seen Jessica playing hopscotch at about eight. She put the later noise down to kids."

"Hopscotch? How old is she?"

"Twenty-two."

Owen raised his eyebrows. "If my memory serves me well, I've seen that name on Sadie's list of friends. Before you go organise a call. Send Nixon. I want it checking. We also may know where she works, probably on her social media profile, we'll have that recorded. Check it. I want to speak to this friend who rang and I want to do that within the next hour. I don't care where the meeting takes place."

"Shall we house check the area?"

Owen paused. He could not justify that expense on one indeterminate phone call. "The two officers you send, get them to ask those within the block. Tell them to look to see who has door cameras and make a note and get any who have saved the recorded images from last night. Thanks, Richard."

Cyril was already in his office. Owen leaned on the door architrave and Cyril continued to view the screen.

"You'll have heard, Owen?" Cyril turned and looked over the top of his glasses. "What are you doing about it?"

"Sent two, one being Nixon to check her apartment and organised to speak with the person who called it in. You think it's connected?" Owen could sense it to be a fact from his boss's position and concentration on the screen.

"Been friends some time, school days although there's a three-year age difference. Why? They might have been at the same school but not in the same class. Also, one works in a cafe and the other is a dental nurse. I know it's a

118

presumption to differentiate work with academic ability but …" For the first time Cyril looked at his colleague. "Quite disparate in many ways. Neither is known to us." Cyril pointed to Owen's jacket. "You need to buy a lottery ticket, my friend, as it looks as though you've been dumped on by a bird!"

Owen looked at the shoulder area to his right and laughed. "No, Christopher's goodbye milky dribble unfortunately. Thought I'd got it all. Do we know much about the family?"

"According to what's come through her parents live in Netherthong just outside …"

"Huddersfield, sir."

For the first time Owen had demonstrated some geographical knowledge, an unusual trait. His interruption still brought a frown to Cyril's face.

"Mmm! Right – makes a change. Quite well off. He's a dentist, the cosmetic side. The flat's in their name. They're coming up today. They've not heard from her for over a week and although according to them that's not unusual, they'd heard about Sadie and were anxious. Apparently, they've met Sadie. Father performed some dental correction work for free." He looked at Owen with an expression that could be interpreted in many different ways but to a DI there was only one conclusion that could be made.

"You don't think he performed in any other way?"

"Open mind, Owen, open mind. Every scenario for her absence should be considered but then you know that. Let's hope he's a man with a generous spirit and nothing more."

"If they were so concerned, why didn't they contact her?" Owen moved near to the desk and sat.

"Apparently, they did. I've requested phone records through Smirthwaite." Those details would give a clear indication of communications over the last twelve months but he doubted he would need to investigate so far into the past. "However, like Sadie, she might have another phone."

As if on cue, Cyril's phone rang.

"Bennett." He turned to Owen. "She's arrived. Take April with you."

Kerry Blake sat in the reception area. The door at the far end clicked and April emerged. It was clear from her posture that she was not only feeling anxious about her visit but concerned for her friend. A man of about her age whom April presumed to be her boyfriend, sat next to her. His hand rested on her knee. Neither spoke. April approached and smiled a welcome.

"Ms Blake?"

Kerry looked immediately at her boyfriend and then at April nodding as she did so.

"Will you come this way, please. Thanks for coming." Her voice was soft and reassuring. "The gentleman may come too. I understand how uncomfortable situations like this can be. It can appear a little daunting." She flashed a smile again once settled in the Interview Room. Owen entered. The introductions were swift and the informality seemed to relieve the stress.

***

Nixon parked to the front of the apartments and checked the address on the scrap of paper he held. He took a moment to scan the area. "Quiet!" He looked at his colleague before opening the door. "We need to chat to a Sarah Hardy, flat 9."

As Harry crossed the open ground, he saw the hopscotch squares. "Not seen one of those for a while." His colleague showed little interest.

Finding the correct buzzer for Hardy's flat he pressed and waited. After a brief conversation the exterior door clicked as the lock was released. They were soon entering.

"Are you sure I can't make you tea?" It was the second time she had asked since they had entered. "Lovely girl, Jess, really thoughtful and a bit of a free spirit. Saw her playing hopscotch in her glad rags last night about eight. Made me laugh out loud. I might have a go tomorrow." She laughed again. "She's not like many young women you meet these days, always has a ready smile and a wave. Carries my bags too if she sees me struggling. Is she alright?"

"What did she do after the hopscotch?" Nixon leaned forward his hands clasped in front across his knees.

"She crossed the grass and headed for the road. I assumed she had a date. Pretty girl. Dentist I think, or one of them people who uses that pipe to suck the water when you're having treatment. I hate the dentist at the best of time but she's a sweetie."

"Did you see anyone else when she was – playing?"

Sarah pulled a face and brought a finger to her chin. "You know, there was."

Chapter 18

The scalpel blade ran down from the nape of Jessica's neck to her waist as the material of her top was lifted away from her body leaving just her bra in place. She moved her head from side to side but could see nothing. The tape across her mouth was uncomfortable and the side of her head throbbed. It felt tight as if blood had congealed in her hair.

"It's like peeling fruit, Jessica. I'll not cut you if you remain still."

She struggled on hearing her name but her arms and legs were bound at the wrist and ankles. He held the blade away waiting for her to calm down. "Not long now." The words came gently as did the blade running down each sleeve, then through the rear waistband of her leggings before the blade ran down each leg revealing her pale flesh. He left on her underwear; after all, he was not a pervert.

Straddling her body, his knees to either side, he rested gently on her buttocks. She felt the heat of panic surge; she feared the worst. Instinctively she stiffened. She could move only her feet and the weight compressed her chest. The blade sliced the plastic tie and each wrist was brought above her head. He lay on her back. He could smell her hair, the same scent he had followed but now there was a tinge of ammonia, of sweat or was it just fear? Applying more of his weight onto her back brought a further tightness to her chest, her head was now trapped. Her respiration became laboured as she could only breathe through her nose made difficult by the constant dribble of mucus.

"Trust me, Jessica, I will not touch you inappropriately and this will take but a few seconds."

Hearing her name again she struggled even more but her efforts were to no avail.

"Shh! We're nearly done."

Her wrists were quickly bound again with the plastic ties, her arms pointing forwards above her head forming a peak along the ground. She looked like a person about to dive into a pool, narrow and arrow straight.

"Thank you." He rolled away and rested momentarily before getting to his feet. "We're done for now."

He watched as her shoulders heaved and he knew she was sobbing. Collecting her clothing, he added it to a charity bag.

***

Owen looked at them both and could see their discomfort and worry but said nothing.

"We met by chance, really, The Winter Gardens, it's convenient for her, she goes often."

"Was she alone?" Owen spoke for the first time.

"Yes, 'I was hoping I'd bump into someone', were her first words. Colin, my fella ..." she turned momentarily to him and then looked back at April, "... was with me for the first hour but he had to leave, he had a family problem and I'd have gone home too had it not been for Jessica."

Owen looked at her partner. "Does Colin have a

surname?"

"Colin Whiers, sorry." She squeezed his hand. "She seemed fine and we had two or three drinks. She mentioned an incident at work, something to do with a bird watcher, 'Twitchers', she said too but to be honest it went over my head. Anyway, when we left, she seemed anxious but not for her, more for me, although the more I think about it the more I feel I was wrong thinking that. It was as if she didn't want to be alone, didn't want to separate. I suggested she call a taxi but she wouldn't have it." She paused as if uncertain about proceeding. "Do you ever miss cues that people offer that are masked by a façade?"

April let the question run and said nothing, her vocabulary seemed puzzling, possibly rehearsed.

"The more I thought about it when I got home, the more I believe I could see behind her false smile."

"Did you call her?"

Kerry shook her head as she turned to Colin who spoke for the first time.

"She sent me a text really early this morning. I was already at work and they don't like personal phones. I'm a chef, breakfast and lunch shift at the moment. I suggested she call Jessica if she was so anxious and she did. She sent me another text saying she couldn't make contact. That's when she went to the flat, I suggested she go."

Kerry nodded. "I was really concerned. It was like seeing pieces of a jigsaw I believed fit together only to watch them crumble! With Sadie still missing I just had to call you. I didn't really know what to do next. I felt guilty about not walking her home or ..."

Colin slipped his arm around her shoulders. "I should be

working now but I've managed to move shifts. She wanted me here, needed me with her."

"Where do you work?" Owen did not look up as he posed the question.

"The Crown Hotel. Have done for two years now."

Owen immediately turned to April.

***

Nixon stood at the patio window of the flat and moved the net curtains to one side. On the narrow balcony a mass of pot plants blocked the view directly below. He could see the row of garages and just make out the hopscotch square. "So, you saw her playing hopscotch and then?"

"She picked up her bag and went through there." She pointed to the sloping roadway to the side of the last garage. "It drops onto Hampsthwaite Road and then to the main road. I assumed she was heading into town. She could go through Luchon Way but a young woman on her own might feel safer on the roads. The car was there." She pointed to the road.

"And it left soon after Jessica?"

"Yes, within a minute. And before you ask it was a dark colour. Strangely I never heard it start or drive away. You do sometimes. Mind, the windows were closed but still I thought it odd. Usually some of the cars round here sound like bloody tanks. Boy racers, I call them."

"The noise you heard at about 11pm?"

"Something must have woken me. I was nodding in this chair. It was like a car door banging. I switched the light off, I only had the reading lamp on and looked through the curtains but there was nothing. If it were by the front door, I wouldn't be able to see and I certainly wasn't going out.

Sometimes taxis stop there. Heard nothing after that."

"Does she have a partner, boyfriend?" Harry asked whilst returning to his seat.

"Did a while back. He stayed quite a lot at weekends or she didn't come home some nights. Haven't seen one recently. A couple of girlfriends but to be honest it's none of my business."

***

Sipping a mug of coffee, he watched the bacon twist in the hot pan. There was something about flesh frying that fascinated. He had frayed the edges of the rashers with scissors and each crenellated edge curled and burned releasing whisps of smoke towards the extractor fan. Heavy scratching in the cage to his left briefly drew his attention. The hamster appeared from the open-ended tube. It brought a smile. "You're wondering what's going on, Lord Byron, aren't you? For such a little creature you are extremely nosey. A lot has gone on, a lot let me tell you."

He cast his mind back six hours. Putting the girls into the tubes was quite easy once he had applied a little liquid soap to the tube's inner surface. It would have appeared to an onlooker like a reverse birth. The twinwall drainage tube's opening was only forty-five centimetres in diameter, but by elongating the victim's posture narrowing their frame, it enabled them to be eased into the confined space. The fact that the inner surface was smooth helped in the process. Jessica had been the easier of the two. Placing her feet against a wall her arms were inserted. He then moved the tube and rotated it to swallow arms, head and shoulders. From past experience, the breasts could be a problem but again, lifting the body and sliding the tube overcame that difficulty. It was now a case of reaching in from the top and taking hold of a hand whilst pulling with one and pushing the rim of the rigid tube with the other. This not so simple manoeuvre allowed the black snake to metaphorically eat its prey. Once the feet were in, the base cap could be fitted temporarily and the whole tube could be stood on its end. A rigid body is far easier to handle than a flaccid, dead weight. Moving the frame into position, he lowered the tube. The external corrugations allowed it to be easily secured. It sat at an angle like some bizarre torpedo tube set away from the floor. He removed the base cap and placed the absorbent pads in readiness to catch any bodily fluids that were sure to come. The final job of the evening was squeezing the Superglue between her shoulders and the inner surface. That would soon set and stop any resistance but there was not much space for any movement. Like Sadie, she had tried to wriggle but she had soon calmed.

It was after breakfast that he looked into the tube's open mouth. Jessica was awake. She could see the circle of artificial light that filtered into the cocoon. The smell of bacon, more a clawing stench, came with the light and attacked her partly constricted nostrils. Tears rolled down her cheeks.

"Jessica, good morning. Can you smell the bacon? I can remove the tape from your mouth if you promise not to scream or shout. Would you like me to do that?"

She nodded frantically. Leaning in he carefully tore the tape away from her lips and the sound of her inhaling more air was abnormally loud. "You will be fine if you stay calm."

Sitting next to the empty plate was her mobile phone. It

was switched off and would remain so. He had no use of her contacts' list. She would be his last friend for a while.

"Soon Jess, may I call you, Jess?" He did not wait for a response. "Soon you'll be with Sadie. You'll like that, Jess, you'll like that."

Chapter 19

Jessica's parents sat opposite Cyril, they looked younger than he had expected but then most people did these days. Both had refused coffee.

"Have you still failed to find Sadie Vance?" Jessica's father's opening gambit was direct and could be said to demonstrate his lack of confidence in the man sitting opposite him even though they had only just met.

"The investigation's still ongoing." Cyril's answer was deliberately short.

"Tell me, Detective Chief Inspector, how seriously are you taking my daughter's disappearance?" He glanced at his wife and then back at Cyril. His hands shook slightly, whether through fear or anger was difficult to discern.

"Many people go missing every year, I'm sure you're aware of that, but a large percentage of these known cases is neither sinister nor deliberate. Others just leave work or home after a domestic incident and are sheltered by friends and family. Every missing person is placed within a continuum of risk and considering the circumstances surrounding your daughter's disappearance, we are treating it as high risk. So according to that policy, owing to your daughter and, we believe, you as a family knowing Sadie, we have set a team working with the utmost priority. For your information, as we sit here the officers are at present searching Jessica's apartment, others are speaking with witnesses whilst the other investigation is ongoing. I've organised a Family Liaison Officer to support you. They will be responsible for maintaining a clear link between us to keep you informed and to ensure nothing is overlooked. We have procedures and we're following them to the letter."

"So, our daughter is at serious risk?" Mrs White's question was uttered with some hesitancy.

"As I've explained, we're treating it as such and hence the influx of officers. We need to establish her immediate whereabouts. We know some of her last known movements. Her photograph and description have been circulated on our website and throughout social media as well as to local partners." Cyril deliberately avoided the word *hospitals* but mentioned taxi firms and transport systems or the fact they were holding off from the use of radio and television appeals. "Her friend has supplied an up-to-date photograph. We're looking into her social media accounts to understand who was on her friends' list and to find those with whom she's been communicating over the last few weeks and more importantly, days. We are and we shall continue to work hard to find your daughter. One thing we must keep in our thoughts when hypothesising the possible reasons for her disappearance, is that your daughter has a right to privacy and therefore does not have to inform family or friends of her whereabouts." This last sentence seemed cold and yet Cyril knew it to be a vital consideration when investigating any missing person.

"All we know is both Jessica and her friend have gone missing. Now whether they've just taken off together or there's something more sinister I cannot say at this stage but I know Jess and she's always been a loving girl who shared her life and her experiences. She's always on the blasted phone and would never turn it off. There are for me, Chief Inspector Bennett, too many elements that do not stack up, they contradict the daughter we know, her foibles and characteristics. I for one don't believe they've gone off together."

Cyril knew this to be the case. The stored information of Sadie's financial data showed she had not touched the meagre account she held and a Financial Investigation Officer was now dedicated to shedding light on Jessica's bank details. Cyril's main concern was that there had been no proof-of-life evidence for Sadie other than the initial received text messages. All other areas of investigation had gone quiet. There had been no definitive, confirmed sightings that could be corroborated with pictorial evidence.

"One final question. Was she seeing anyone – romantically?" Cyril now found this a difficult question to ask considering the endless possibilities. He noticed the mother squeeze her partner's hand and the immediate change to her expression highlighted a concern.

"Not since the last. She was hurt badly, not only emotionally but financially. Initially, she was blind to the problem but we noticed it, she changed over the relationship. You can advise and support your children but they have to see the situation for what it is, perceive it how we and her friends saw it."

"Do you have his name and know where he is now?" Cyril picked up his pen.

"Robert Ashman, she always called him Rob. From

131

what we heard he disappeared to Scotland, working in the wind turbine industry. We were told he was a pipeline engineer, laying the conduit that carries cables and such. He worked away a lot. I feel it was an apocryphal tale concocted by a total philanderer and user. To be blunt, he emptied her account and added considerably to her credit card bills."

"Is she still in financial trouble?" He had known a number of cases who had resorted to suicide, not only through debt but the emotional trauma of a soured relationship.

"No, she has a loving family who were in a position to help, thank goodness. I know what you're thinking but Jess is stronger than that. There's something I think we should share with you. Jess had a problem when she was at Primary School, we were going through a difficult patch." He paused and glanced at his wife. "It was all my fault and the situation brought about a sudden change in Jess, her behaviour changed, deteriorated. To cut a long story short she was excluded from school after a number of failed interventions. Anyway, she attended a special school, Fellside, EBD it was the closest to our home. You're aware of EBD? I hurt them both through my selfish ways."

"Children with emotional and behavioural difficulties but I doubt they carry that title now."

"Indeed." He paused as if drawing deeply from within his memory, a memory that was painful yet liberating. "Anyway, her behaviour seemed to deteriorate further for a few months. She also had a dreadful, surly attitude to us at home but then within a few days, after returning from the half-term break, she suddenly started to revert to her old self. We were told she'd befriended another girl who'd just arrived in the same class and they also had a new class teacher. It was like a lightbulb being switched on and she suddenly emerged from out of the shadows."

Cyril scribbled the word, *shadows,* it seemed to appear more and more throughout the investigation.

"Within a year she was back, back in mainstream education and she didn't dip again. Mind, neither did we." He looked towards his wife an element of guilt clearly trapped within his expression.

***

Owen sat with Carruthers, the missing person investigating officer, and April. Nixon had called for a CSI team to search the front of Jessica's apartment. They would take prints and DNA samples too from within. Any IT equipment would be removed for investigation. He had already police-taped an area ensuring it allowed for ingress and exit of those still within the building, but protecting the areas identified as being relevant to the case. He now also knew the names of the residents from received intelligence that he had requested. Once another colleague arrived, he would work door-to-door within the building.

Cyril arrived at the meeting within minutes. He dropped the file he held onto the table but deliberately failed to make eye contact with any of the team.

"Considering the circumstances the parents find themselves in they were remarkably calm. The management meetings are now a joint affair but I feel and I'm sure so too does Owen, that we have a compelling degree of evidence to link the two girls. April you will take SIO of the Jessica case and Owen, continue that of Sadie until we have firm proof that ..." He did not finish his sentence. "What do we have?"

April tapped the piece of paper in front of her as she looked at Cyril. "The Crown Hotel has come up again. Carl Guy, the chap who supposedly found the scooter, worked there and so too we discover today does the boyfriend of the girl interviewed a while ago who was the last to see Jessica. His name is Colin Whiers and he's a chef. You recall, Carl would go early and have breakfast in the kitchen."

"Keep that back from the public at the moment. Organise an interview with him at his home address. Don't meet him at work. I also want the ex-boyfriend, the one who emptied her accounts. We have a name, Robert Ashman. I've started the search so we should hear soon."

***

April stood on the steps of the dental practice along with Jessica White's colleague, Connie Ashcroft. Neither spoke for a few moments as April scanned the area.

"You mentioned the person watching from across the road?"

Connie had wrapped her arms around herself as if forming a shield, her body language could only be described as defensive against something she could not see. "I was upstairs and Jess was close to where you are now. I saw her check her phone but it was only for seconds. It was then I saw him, concealed and holding either binoculars or a telescope. I said it was a spyglass to Jess." She paused. "It made her laugh and I felt foolish. She'd been looking at a bird, it was beautiful and she dismissed the man as a bird watcher. I guess having the vast area of

134

The Stray, Harrogate sees its fair share of unusual birds."

"What made you look out at that moment? Did you know Jess was outside?"

"No, it was the sound of the sirens, there seemed so many. They were attending the hit and run by the station I discovered later."

"So, when did he go?"

"As soon as I arrived here, one minute he was there, the next he'd gone."

"Let's walk over the road and I want you to show me the precise position."

Within the hour the area had been cordoned off and a PCSO monitored the site until a CSI unit arrived. If luck was with them there could be visible evidence left and April was optimistic that footwear analysis might find something.

Chapter 20

The hamster spun within the wheel and the generated buzzing noise seemed constant. There was the occasional movement within the black cylinder just behind, drawing his attention away from the hamster. The absorbent pads beneath the lower opening had been changed twice.

"You must be thirsty, Jess." He heard her begin to cry again. Leaning in he passed a tube between her stretched arms and placed the mouthpiece to her lips. The other end of the tube was attached to a runner's hydration rucksack. She drank and all noise ceased momentarily.

"Why? I can hear your thoughts as you drink. You're wondering why you're here? What have I done they whisper to me? Who is doing this? These are all relevant questions any intelligent human being would ask, they're all reasonable and all in need of answers. Spit out the tube when you've had enough. It's because of what you represent. I really don't know you. I've seen your pictures. I think I know your friends in a way people know and collect friends on social media. They're not real are they? They're just a name and a photograph. We trust too easily. I trusted, just as you have done, trusted people whom I believed had my best interests at heart, that they could and would help but when push comes to shove …" He tapped the cylinder.

"They lied. Goodness, we did a fair bit of that to get you where you are now, pushing and shoving, I mean. Anyway, all too often these people fail you. In my experience, Jess, the majority of those who have fitted into that category throughout my life have been female. I seemed to be surrounded by them."

Jessica tried to hit the inner side of the cylinder with her bound hands. "Help me, please, help me."

"See, like those of whom I speak you're the same, you're not listening. Hearing but not heeding. There was never empathy. Alas, it was ever thus. It's all about them – the words, later, not now, another time, when I've done this – it was rarely, how can I help you?" His outburst grew more emotional and there was evidently a degree of resentment. He leaned on the cylinder. Jessica could sense his distress.

Recovering, he approached the cupboard, removed an end cap for the cylinder and collected the contact adhesive. Within minutes the lower opening had been sealed. The light within diminished proportionately. Jessica looked up into the remaining light.

As she glanced up at the opening, a silhouetted head appeared. "Selfish you see, you're just like the rest, like Sadie. It's all about you, isn't it? Let's play a little game my sweet hopscotch girl. You'll know it – I Spy with my Little Eye. Why didn't you stop Sadie doing what she was doing? You were, I believe real friends and not just names on Facebook. I've seen the pictures. You knew her boyfriend rather well. She told me that, she'd tell me anything I wanted to know before she left and went away. However, Jessica," he spit out the word with a measure of disgust, "I don't need to know anything from you as I have no more to gain from any of your friends. You're not going to answer me, are you?"

"I don't know, he was a friend. It was just a couple of times."

"I knew it! She didn't really tell me anything. Her asthma. I guessed. Snippets from Facebook are the metaphorical keys to your lives and … It's now time. Goodnight, Jess and as my mother would say, *don't let the bed-bugs bite*."

"Please! I'm sorry! I don't understand what I'm supposed to have done to you. I don't know who you are."

The smell of the glue flooded the cylinder stinging her nostrils. It was pungent and was an excuse for more tears. Within seconds all light had gone.

"See, Lord Byron, they never listen, they only think of themselves. I think I need tea. Why is the youth of today so gullible?"

***

The group within the management meeting had considered the latest information. Photographs taken from the dental practice window of the alleged site where the suspect loitered were added to the board alongside details of the forensic evidence retrieved from the apartment building. April opened the proceedings.

"We have collected her electronic tablet and there's no other storage device. Interestingly, in the area close to the apartment's entrance CSI discovered fragments from what they believe to be a cardboard tube, the type found in the centre of household goods like cling film or foil. Not your loo rolls, they say they're too flimsy. They're confident there is blood trace, human hair and some skin found trapped within the card's residue. It's under analysis and we should know soon if it matches that of Jessica White. We have her DNA from her hairbrush as well as a very grainy image of a dark coloured vehicle parked near the group of garages. The site is close to where a pedestrian would walk on approaching the flat's entrance from the road. Sadly, we have no registration number. If this car belongs to the suspect, then they'd have known the direction in which she was approaching and therefore they'd be following or even anticipating her arrival. Forewarned is forearmed. How she was taken at this stage, if she were taken, can only be surmised but we have to use the evidence we have at our disposal. Forensics have collected some shoe impressions from the area in which the suspect was seen observing the dental practice along with some paper tissue caught on one of the bushes."

April looked at each of the members around the table.

"Let's just make a few intelligent guesses, brain storm it used to be called. Let's imagine our suspect has been watching Jessica for some time. He knows where she lives, her place of work, maybe some of her friends, how she travels between home and work. He might even have followed her on occasion, even when she went to The Winter Gardens. We know the approximate time of her arrival and departure."

A voice from within the group was eager to respond. "Stalker?"

April raised her shoulders. "Infatuation as we know can be the catalyst to murder. Harry, pay the pub a visit after you've requested CCTV from the place. Collect any CCTV of the route to and from her home on that night wherever possible. You have a time scale to work to. Do that now, please."

Harry collected his notes and left the room.

"She returns home and our suspect has been waiting. He's known where she's been, he knows her route." She noticed a few raised eyebrows. "Just stick with this hypothesis a while longer. What's the light situation like around the apartment block at the approximate time she returned? Check it."

Shakti entered. "We've located the boyfriend who her parents say robbed her blind, Robert Ashman. He's working now as a wind turbine technician at Crystal Rig windfarm in the Scottish Borders. I've requested support from Police Scotland regarding basic information until we can get someone there. Its twenty miles or so from Dunbar where most of the technicians are based. It's believed he lives there."

"Excellent. Thank you. One for Smirthwaite as soon as. Where did he live when he was here in Harrogate?"

Shakti supplied the information.

"Usually at White's address. He's been a bit of a butterfly has our Rob, bit of an opportunist when it comes to sleeping arrangements. He travelled with his work and took opportunities when they arose, but according to Jessica's parents he lived with his mother. I'm tracking his history and will let you know. Nomads are obviously never easy to locate."

***

Owen contemplated the street map showing the area in which Sadie had been spotted. The one location that did not fit the general pattern was the sighting of the scooter on

Skipton Road. His phone rang. The cafe owner was put through.

"DI Owen? It's Lindsey Aitchison from the cafe. Something's been bothering me since our chat the other day. You had to leave when you received a phone call and we were very busy if you remember." She paused.

"Yes, sorry. Still no good news to report."

"I'm so worried. That's partly the reason I called. Stef, the girl you met working with me, well she told me that she believed Sadie was meeting someone behind her boyfriend's back. A no mark, as she referred to him, bit of a Jack the Lad. It was what she'd heard and I was going to mention it but time got the better of us ... Anyway, late yesterday a customer came in, it was Frank, I mentioned him, he was on the list. He always commented on the smell of bacon but never bought any."

"I remember, you thought he read poetry and looked like a tramp. Dead bird and nest." It brought a smile on reflection of that. "Go on."

"We were chatting about this and that and he mentioned he'd seen Sadie on the day she went missing. She was in the grave yard of St John's Church on Crab Lane."

"Church?" Owen glanced at the street map and ran his finger from her last known location to the church. That was the direction in which she appeared to be heading. "Go on."

"Frank apparently takes flowers for his wife. I don't know if she's buried there or just in the memorial garden, I didn't ask as he didn't say. Anyway, he mentioned that he gets the 2B bus into town from the Crab Lane post office after his visit. When he saw Sadie, she was with a man, he thought older than her but he couldn't be one hundred percent certain. He didn't say much else. I thought it was vital you know."

Owen finished taking notes. "It's crucial and couldn't have come at a better time. I need to chat to Frank. Any idea where he lives?"

"I'll find out and get back to you." She hung up.

Within minutes a car had been sent to the church with instructions to assess the situation and also to question the owner of the post office. If his wife were buried there, Frank might well live close by and if anyone knew him from the vivid description given by the cafe owner, then those in the post office would. A search of CCTV in the specific area was instigated as a matter of urgency. He surmised that most churches would now have some kind of security system owing to the number of lead thefts. Owen Googled the church. The details of the website appeared and although he found a contact number, he had some difficulty locating a name.

"Is that the Rector? The is DI Owen from Harrogate police. You may have seen or read about the local girl, Sadie Vance, who's gone missing?" He had. "We've reason to believe that she was seen within the grounds of St John's on the day of her disappearance. She was seen by an elderly gentleman by the name of Frank. I believe his wife is either buried there or she rests within the memorial garden." The term sounded clumsy but was hopefully sensitively worded.

"I think I know the man to whom you're referring, Inspector. His name is Frank but ..." he paused. "How do I know that you're a member of the police and that you are who you say you are? We get so many calls these days where the caller purports to be someone they're not."

"If you would please contact Harrogate Police station and ask for me they will put you through. DI David Owen. Say it's urgent and that I'm expecting your call. I'll let you find the number."

"We have the number at hand these days, it's now, sadly, an unacceptable fact of life."

Within a matter of minutes Owen's phone rang. "DI Owen."

"You are who you say you are. I'm sorry, but you can never be too careful. The gentleman is Franklyn Moffett, he does like to be called Frank. His wife passed away only a short time ago. How may I help?"

"Do you have his address?"

"I do, yes, but I would prefer for him to contact you. I shall call him and stress the urgency. Mr Moffett may give the wrong first impression but he is as bright as a button. He is finding life without his wife rather difficult but he has many friends within the church. If he's seen something you can be assured the report that he will give will be accurate. Is there anything else?"

The efficient, succinct answer was almost clinical in its delivery and Owen was lost for words. "No, no I think you've answered my question fully but there's one other thing. I've sent a car with an officer to take a look around the grounds, he may well be there now. His name is Hall. Do you have any external security cameras in place?"

"That's fine. We do, but only two. They're placed to observe the entrances to the building. We have to balance privacy with security within the church you understand. I'll pop over to see if I can see the officer and give any assistance I can but I'll contact Franklyn first. I'm sure he'll be in touch soon."

Chapter 21

Brian Smirthwaite had received full co-operation from Police Scotland who had, through the local police at Dunbar, made contact with Robert Ashman's latest known employers. He was still in employment and had rental accommodation in Dunbar, some twenty-one miles from Crystal Rig One wind farm where he worked a varying shift pattern and had done so for eight months. Brian also received an employee assessment for that period which was impressive. He organised to travel by train from York the following day and Ashman would be present at the local police station for his anticipated arrival. His employer was made aware of the facts surrounding the request and was fully supportive. Ashman would be informed on the day of the meeting.

***

The cylinder had been loaded into the back of the estate car and covered with a blanket. Three cement bags were also stacked on a plastic sheet. For the first time since beginning this quest, he felt anxious about the location he had chosen for the drop. He had searched Google maps so often, a degree of uncertainty had crept into his mind. As this was the last disposal for some time, he felt a degree of anti-climax but then the silly error with the phone and text message had played on his mind. Switching the phone on, making the call and sending a text, from that place, an unfamiliar location to the girl, had been a foolish thing to do and he had reprimanded himself. He was aware that simple mistakes would be all they would need to track him, find him and then punish him, lock him away. That could never be allowed to happen.

He would go and assess the potential of both venues, qualify his original reasoning and then and only then would he make his decision. The journey would be done in daylight and once the final decision had been made, he would drive and get a coffee somewhere, maybe Pateley Bridge. He could park and walk, wait for the light to fade and return to the chosen location safe in the knowledge it was the right choice.

***

True to her word, April searched the previous missing person files concentrating not only on those females who had not been found but also on those who had. That proved far too broad a search so she removed the ones who had been found alive. She was aware this might compromise the logic of her initial idea but practicality and time had to influence the investigation and this thought process. The criteria she now applied was deliberately narrow and steered by the details she had of the latest missing women – their general build, their size, height, ethnicity. She added their ages. She gave the search an age category of between eighteen years and twenty-five. To her surprise, thirty-one cases came up, more than she had anticipated. From these she graded them by location, initially splitting the north and south of England before narrowing those in the north to within set distances from Harrogate. There was no sound nor scientific reason but one based purely on logical thought. If this person had kidnapped and killed before, had previous history, there was a greater likelihood of the cases being within the same area.

She also felt a need to add the date the victims went missing and for some, the date their bodies had been located. This element was crucial. There would be a location A and B in some cases. That distance could aid the present investigation considerably. The computer allowed her to tag and annotate this information onto a nationwide map that was visible on an interactive board. From what she could initially ascertain, there was clearly no pattern other than the majority went missing within the larger urban conurbations and yet bodies linked to a certain number of those cases were found in what might be described as rural locations.

"Seven years," she announced to nobody as she was alone in the room. She stood, arms folded, staring at the map. "What will that leave?"

Adding the information brought a further reduction but also showed a concentration within a one-hundred-mile radius of Harrogate, the largest group being in Humberside. There would, she knew only too well, be similarities to the present case. She focused on those found and the injuries they had sustained.

***

DC Hall had chatted to the Rector for longer than he had anticipated. The recordings taken from the church cameras did not go back far enough and he was told in no uncertain terms that he, as Rector, had the right to set that storage time: there was no law specifying the storage of digital footage for churches and data protection he considered to be a serious matter; there had to be a balance.

The post office too had thrown data protection regulations at him as he requested the information. To Hall this was an irony as he recalled that a while back the Post Office scandal had ruined many lives and torn families apart because of a fault in a new IT system. Many working behind the counters were accused of theft, fraud and false accounting.

He called Owen's mobile. "Nothing. It's quite a large graveyard and there's like a private road leading to the church. If, as we believe, she came on the scooter it could have been parked anywhere. However, my guess is Bilton Road."

"I'm awaiting a call from Mr Moffett. I'm assured he's on the ball with things. Come back and add your finding ..." Owen's desk phone rang. "This is probably him." He hung up and collected the other phone.

"DI Owen."

"Sorry, it's the Rector. Did he ring?"

The conversation was brief. "I must insist on his address. We have a young woman whose life might be in danger and time waits for no one, particularly if they ..." he didn't finish.

Within minutes he was heading for the car, the address added to a piece of paper. He knew just where it was.

***

The cases had been coded into SCAS and comparative cases would be analysed. April also worked independently. Strangulation, rape, drowning, severe beatings, the injuries resulting in the cause of death were disturbing, and in some cases totally barbaric and brutal. There were, however, four deaths where blunt instrument trauma to the side of the head was noted but according to the autopsy results this was not the cause of death; their deaths were a result of asphyxia. However, further more accurate cases were discovered by the SCAS indexers using their database. Four relevant victims had been found, one had her head wrapped in cling film whilst others were discovered bound and gagged. Traces of cardboard and circular bruising were found in the area of the trauma on one victim, suggesting a severe strike by a tube. None of the four had any other injuries and none had been sexually assaulted. Two were fully clothed but two were found wearing only underwear; none wore shoes. She checked the photographic records of each case. The date from their going missing to the time they were found varied broadly but two were within a year – two months was the shortest time and the other was over two years. The file from SCAS was circulated within the team. The name of the serious crime analyst linked to the findings was added to the board.

April sat and rested her face in her hands, cupping her eyes and gently massaging them before staring back at the display boards. She looked at the word *penumbra* and read the meaning Shakti had included. "A peripheral or indeterminate area or group." She thought for a while. *If I were to describe it, it would be a shadow hiding within another shadow, a half shadow.* Moving her hand to her mouth she remembered something from a conversation whilst teaching at Sunday school. Ironically, it was a lightbulb moment. She left the room heading for her desk. She needed her Bible and would then locate Shakti.

***

The car park positioned above the road, aptly named Reservoir Road, was quiet but then it was midweek; there were on this occasion few sightseers. The view towards the dam wall was perfect. There was no public transport to the location but the area was a favourite for walkers and picnickers. He had walked it himself many times and he knew it could be busy when the weather was fine.

Leaving the car, he swung his fleece over his shoulder. The sun when released from behind the white cumulus clouds, was hot. Within five minutes he stood looking at the downslope of the dam, the overflow side. Water ran in a layer, a constant rush of what seemed like white, boiling turbulence that cascaded down the spillway.

Climbing before swinging his legs over the broad parapet, he let them dangle over the void. The view now was dizzying and it brought a strange feeling within the pit of his stomach. It was neither fear nor pleasure, more a natural warning of potential danger. The breeze channelled up the valley collected and delivered some fine spray against his face. He closed his eyes. There was something about being up high where the perspective of the world was brought into clear focus. Carefully he got to his feet, pointed his hands to the sky and let the breeze sway his body. How different this felt from sitting. It made him feel more courageous. Taking a deep breath, he swung his legs and jumped onto the road. The view of the spillway was not the side of the dam he wanted to study. He needed water, water that was dark and deep.

Crossing the narrow road, he again leaned on the opposite parapet and stared down at the stonework that held the huge weight of water. This water flooded the valley and stretched blue, a magic, liquid mirror that exaggerated the colour of the sky way into the distance. He had no idea of its depth especially at the dam wall but here the water held the colour of the night. It was dark and with that a feeling of cold enveloped him and he assumed the water to be at its greatest depth.

He circled his eyes with his now-binocular hands and allowed his view to skim just above the watery blue. Suddenly, the idea of the Dam Busters came into his mind and he could imagine aircraft dropping to disturb the flat, glossy surface. The night sky would have been clear and the moon bright, reflecting galleon-like before frightened flyers released the cylinder-shaped bombs in the hope they would skip and bounce like pebbles. The idea of them hitting the wall and then sinking before exploding brought his own cylinder to mind. Like the bombers, it would be here, late that night when he could roll the weighted cylinder off this very wall, the wall he now casually leaned on. It would fall into the darkness, black into black, before hitting the water. Would it float? That was the fear. Or would it linger momentarily before filling and sinking to be lost in the cold and the dark? Doubt suddenly filled his mind. He could not be sure and he needed certainty. He had the cement and surely that would do the trick.

A buzzing sound broke his concentration. It was faint at first but then grew more audible. Hearing its whine but not seeing it, he searched to find the source. Looking back towards the car park he noticed someone standing on a picnic table, he was looking towards the dam. It was then he saw the drone; it caught the sun for a second and flashed a giveaway signal. His eyes tracked it as it dropped over the overflow side of the dam. He crossed quickly to watch it follow the water before rising to climb back towards the person in the car park.

On his return, the drone pilot was still there. The machine rested on the table next to the hand control and thermos flask. He was drinking coffee and checking the video footage he had taken.

"Is it a good day for flying one of those? I could hear it but it took a while to locate it. It's so small!"

"I hope I didn't disturb you. I waited until you put your feet on the road before flying the drone, didn't want to be responsible for you following the same route as the water into the overflow! If you'd like you can see the footage for yourself." He handed over the electronic tablet, the video was still running.

Panic began to flush through his stomach as he watched. He could see himself looking up. The image was sharp and clear. He had a sudden urge to destroy it, throw it as far away as possible or stamp on it, but he knew that would not only be stupid but pointless as the video might already be stored in the digital cloud.

"What wonderful pictures! How sharp for such a small machine."

"They get better and better and cheaper like all technology. I'll send you the footage if you let me have an email address."

Handing back the tablet he shook his head. "Thanks, but no. It's been rewarding and educational but I'll get no pleasure from seeing myself." He chuckled. "Thank you and safe flying." He returned to the car.

Malcolm Hollingdrake

Chapter 22

The joint morning meeting commenced later than planned. A number of elements of the investigation were beginning to bear fruit. The room was busy and April's UK map filled the electronic screen at the far end of the room. The attendance of officers in the room grew, each carried pieces of paper or files. April rearranged her notes and chatted briefly to Owen.

***

Smirthwaite stood by the door of the train as it pulled into Dunbar station. It was not what he had expected and a far cry from the York station he had left a few hours previously. He noticed a uniformed officer leaning against a wall by the only building, his face staring at his phone screen. Occasionally he scanned the alighting passengers with only a cursory glance. As Brian stepped onto the platform the officer stood, slipped his phone into his pocket and approached.

"Even dressed like everyone else you spotted I was police?" Brian's unorthodox greeting brought a smile.

"Nae aye. DC Brian Smirthwaite? I presumed correctly. Ne Scottish magic, I checked your photograph on the system. Saves me staring at everyone who leaves the train and making tongues wag, it doesnae take much in these parts. Good trip?" His rich Scottish brogue tripped from his tongue and Brian had to listen carefully to catch every word.

"Painless, thanks. Contemplated driving but then ..."

"Ashman should be at the station when we arrive. I've contacted them to say you're on time. We didnae want the young Jimmy sweating for too long."

"Jimmy?"

Aye, young Robbie Ashman. The car's here and the police station's a three minute drive away."

Brian smiled hoping the confusion was part of his very early start to the day. The car was parked on the centre of a turning circle on the only road that ended at the stone station building. To their right was the car park. Brian stopped and looked at an impressive church a short distance away to his right; the tower was capped with four tall corner stones, the stone a rich red colour.

"Like the kirk, do ya? Just been all renovated, aye, one of our impressive pieces of Scottish architecture. Not a church man masell but you'll ne be too impressed by the police station, nae like your one in Harrogate. I checked it out too. All fancy technology, I believe, and that's just to keep ya warm!"

He was right. On arrival the station looked more domestic than he could have imagined, the flat roofed extension, rendered in grey pebble dash certainly gave it an air of austerity. The common element, however, was the blue window frames.

"Only opens from nine till five, a cop shop you might say, so we only expect people to break the law during opening hours. Your Jimmy will've been entertained in the interview suite." He winked and pointed to the door. "I'll sort some coffee for ya both, he's had one already but never let them tell ya that we Scots are tight. Informal chat I was told."

"Two sugars would be perfect, thanks."

Robert Ashman sat to one side of a table. One end was fixed to the wall. A bench was positioned to only one side, the side on which he was seated. The bench was connected to the table legs; the furniture was designed to go nowhere. Interview rooms differed little from one station to another but this one took Brian back to his early police career. Usually it was the smell, a mix of disinfectant, stale sweat and fresh air, with the disinfectant usually being the dominant aroma, but this was different.

"Sorry about the stink, I'm guilty of that. Curry last night and it wasn't a particularly good one! Well, it was alright last night but this morning was a different story and as they say, it's better out than in." Ashman pulled the kind of face that was a blend of apology and laddish humour as if he were testing the response.

It was not the welcome Smirthwaite had expected but it certainly was not the first time he had experienced the uncouth youth.

"For someone who works on a wind farm I guess I should have expected nothing less, Mr Ashman."

It brought a belly laugh from Ashman and Brian sensed a degree of relief as he saw the man's shoulders relax. He had broken the ice. Opening the door he propped it with one of the two chairs to keep it ajar before taking the remaining one and sitting.

"That should be better in a few minutes. DC Smirthwaite, Harrogate police. Have they told you why I'm here, Mr Ashman?

"Jess White. She's gone missing." His tone changed and he tensed again. There was a degree of concern in his response. "You've still not found ..." he paused knowing if they had he would not be sitting where he was unless ... "She's alright, isn't she? Safe?"

"No, we haven't. Would you expect that, for her to just go off without telling anyone? We believe that you knew her well and your relationship lasted some time."

"To be honest, no, I don't think she would, that's certainly not her character. She did threaten to throw me out on more than one occasion but for her to go ... no!"

The interview progressed slowly; it was deliberately planned to allow Ashman as much time to talk as possible. Brian took notes on his electronic pad.

"I know I've been a right bastard but addiction is a dreadful mistress. She turns you into a scheming, unreliable liar whilst constantly emptying any pockets you can get your hands into. I have a gambling addiction and I'm not proud I can assure you, it is always here, nagging." He pointed to his temple. "Just one more, it might be the big one. She, my counsellor, that is, put it down to being away from home, travelling, boredom, working with blokes who were addicts themselves in one way or another. My dad was an addict, booze, but he never acknowledged it. Maybe it's in my genes. What do they say, 'Paid on Friday, broke on Saturday?' On many occasions that was me; as I say, I was a right bastard. When I had my weeks at home, at Jess's flat, it didn't stop. I would borrow at first and then take or scrounge. It brought nothing but trouble in the end, rows and fights. I even went with her mates. If I could get into their knickers then I knew I could get into their pockets. So, to answer your question it was me who left – and when I did eventually go, I left her in debt. I like to think I left to protect her but if I'm honest, she had nothing left. Her parents refused to help further and she was financially embarrassed and emotionally broken. I was what you'd call a right Jack the Lad or maybe a better description is a bastard. I know that."

"Did you know Sadie Vance?"

"I did."

"And were her pockets safe?"

"No, but she was a kid and had little. She wanted what I didn't have and that was the ability to make her feel special."

"Did Jessica know?"

Ashman shrugged his shoulders. "I doubt it."

"Have you changed since coming here?" Brian looked directly at Ashman to determine whether his eyes told the same story as his mouth.

"I had to. I'd lost everything apart from my job and I was pretty close to losing that. I decided I needed to be in one place and not chasing around the country. Hotel living sounds great until you do it. First month or two were great with meals provided, some beer money, someone making your bed, the odd woman or two helping financially but it soon wore off. You become nomadic and exceptionally selfish and extremely bored. Many lads I've worked with are too fond of the booze and when you do the job we do, it can be a recipe for disaster. I applied for a fixed position up here away from my past and was fortunate to get it. I guess you could say I've eventually grown up even though I'm the age I am. I needed a clean sheet. You might not believe me but I'm concerned for Jess. She didn't deserve me and she doesn't deserve to be in the predicament she's now in."

Brian looked up on hearing the word 'predicament.'

***

April met her colleagues in the Incident Room. She had slipped the black, thin ribbon between the pages of her Bible and it sat on the desk before her. It had belonged to her mother and she could not remember a time when it was not part of her life. She stood holding a sheet of paper. She began to read:

"'Something that can be important yet easily missed, an outer shadow. Families and loved ones often turn a blind eye because they see the things they don't want to see except briefly. There could be someone out there who she's truly upset, pissed off in that specific moment. Shadows are only here when the sun shines and can soon vanish, we could say they're a bit like our dark moods and uncontrollable emotional outrages, periods of darkness when we might act out of character or some might say, we show our true personality.' These direct notes are taken from the recording when Shakti interviewed Rachel Gaunt who contacted us after our appeal when Sadie first went missing. I believe I'm right in saying Shakti thought she clearly had an axe to grind." She looked at Shakti who responded.

"There was something, I don't know what but there was a resentment, a bitterness. She was angry. It was the word penumbra. I couldn't get the imagery out of my head so consequently I wrote it down." She pointed briefly to the text on the board.

April continued. "It has stuck with me too and after some careful thought I feel it's most relevant to both of these cases. People appear to live one life and only when others look more deeply into those lives do they see within the shadows, see part of the person that is partially hidden by the shade." She tapped a finger reverently on the small Bible. "I've been reading, so do be patient and it will, I hope, make some sort of sense."

There was a degree of movement in the room as people leaned closer in anticipation. Cyril looked on proudly as he remembered introducing April to the team and how she had become a vital part.

"We can often have an inclination of something missing in our lives, I've felt it at times and I'm sure you have too. It's when we're at a low ebb, when something's affected us strongly, the death of a friend, personal failure or just our emotional frame of mind – we're suddenly living in the shadows." She paused and looked at some of the faces to see if what she was saying was making sense to them. "It's what C S Lewis called *The Shadowlands* – having a vague feeling that there's something more. Now, that can be interpreted from the point of view of the person looking out from within the penumbra or from those on the outside looking in. To some those passing shadows are real, but in another ways, they're not. We seek the life where we feel comfortable and hide what we don't want to appear in the light. A denial. Is it possible both women lived part of their lives in the Shadowlands?" There was a prolonged silence. "Am I making any sense?"

It was Cyril who spoke first. "'We live in the Shadowlands – the sun is always shining somewhere else, round the bend in the road, over the brow of the hill.' As you've said, April. C S Lewis."

She smiled, more out of relief. "Yes, and to take the thought a little further, people, particular in their youth, are always looking for something more. Life has been given to them but the opportunity to live it has not or they're denied from progressing for whatever reason."

Owen frowned and rubbed his forehead. The hypothesis had flown well over his head and he sat back in his chair and sighed. "So, if they've both been taken and if we presume by the same person, a person who probably knew them both, do we believe he could see within their shadow world, knew their weaknesses and therefore in some ways had control over them?"

"Or, Owen, they shone a light drawing out his shadows and witnessed his fears."

"Revenge?" someone said from further back in the room.

"Matthew 4:16 'The people who live in the darkness have seen great light and those living in the shadowland of death, light has dawned.' If you can identify and accept your weaknesses there is a greater chance of seeing those weaknesses in others. It therefore becomes a weapon, a strength." April knew she had stretched her point a little too far and turned to the screen before detailing the findings from her research.

On hearing of the evidence linking a cardboard tube with a specific victim from a cold case, there was a sudden surge of enthusiasm. "I've requested an urgent re-analysis of the evidence to see if there's a link. The woman was of a similar build to Sadie and Jessica." She sat down and

Owen moved to the front.

"How do I follow that?" His question was genuine. He looked at April before fumbling with his notes. "Sadie was seen on the day she went missing by a Franklyn Moffett. He knew her fairly well, well enough to make a fuss of her when visiting her place of work, the cafe, so I'm more than comfortable with his evidence. We know she travelled in the area where she was seen on the scooter that day as it was caught on dashcam footage and we have a description of the man she met. There are no images from the security cameras at the church as they're on a short loop. Moffett also believed that they were smoking weed, his words. Mostly her as he'd watched them for some time.

"As you know Brian's having a brief holiday in Scotland." His comment lightened the atmosphere and laughter and banter broke out. "We received a brief, interim report that tells us that Robert Ashman has an addiction to gambling hence Jessica White's financial trouble when he left her. Ashman also had a brief fling with Sadie but more on that to follow. He now seems to be more in control if that's ever possible for a gambler but from what he's said to date, Brian doesn't believe he's our man. He was working when both women went missing. He'll be questioning him further."

Chapter 23

The dark blue Skoda estate was parked in the lower car park at Pateley Bridge. The warden checked the ticket left on the dashboard. There were just under two hours remaining. He could see the passenger seat was folded forward slightly and one of the rear seats had been lowered. Whatever was under the blanket stretched diagonally nearly across the length of the car towards the boot. He had always liked the look of this particular model, the fact that it was hybrid attracted him more. He was determined to keep an eye open for the owner on their return to have a chat, having always believed that it was good to talk to the horse's mouth about all things automotive.

The road leading up towards Pateley Bridge from the river appeared to be squeezed between the buildings as they seemed to overhang the busy strip of tarmac. Each window was a meeting point for sightseers and shoppers; they blocked part of the pavement and slowed the traffic almost to a crawl. The smell of meat pies drifted towards him as he walked up. The nearer the butcher's shop he got, the more his appetite was whetted as the aroma grew in intensity. But the pie could wait, it was a coffee he needed and a place to rethink.

With the final sips of the coffee came his decision. The alternative location was closer to Harrogate but he was more certain the place would still offer the degree of solitude needed. It was not about the body being located, more about the time between deposit and discovery. He reflected on a conversation that informed his judgement. One victim had been located but not for some considerable time, that would be time to start anew, time for the weather to erode any careless and inadvertent clues he might leave. He tried to recall the conversation but he could not even remember her name. He found that best, to push the fine details away into a dark recess of his mind. Checking the time, he needed to be back at the car, he also needed a pie. *It could be worse. I could have been like the cruel Mr Todd, the pie maker.* His inappropriate thought brought a smile but considering the practicalities made him shiver. At least he did not abuse or damage them – he kept them whole.

Crossing the bridge, he stared down at the clear, peaty water of the River Nidd. It was transparent and shallow. A brown trout seemed to hover, camouflaged against the pebbles and stones in the gentle flow. Its motion seemed effortless but it was alert. Reaching the other side, he popped into the public toilets and within minutes he crossed to the car park. As he approached the car he was immediately startled.

"Is that your car?" The voice behind him caused him to pause. Turning slowly, he saw what he assumed to be a traffic warden or parking attendant quickly approaching him. His yellow fluorescent jacket glowed brightly in the afternoon sunshine.

He opened the driver's door, removed the ticket and checked the printed time before glancing at his watch; he had ten minutes remaining. In his defence he held it out to the official. His heart rate increased and he felt a sudden flush of nerves.

"No, no, sorry, you're fine. Time in hand as we say. I've fancied one of these cars since they came out. It's the hybrid bit that confuses me whereas the all-wheel drive appeals. Round the Dales you need that in winter especially on Greenhow Hill yonder." He pointed in the approximate direction. "Bloody steep and when it's been gritted it can be really tricky. I see it can take quite a load. DIY planned?" He pointed to the back of the car.

There was a pause as the bag containing the pie was placed on the remaining rear seat. "I'd recommend it. I'd get one. Thanks for asking but I must fly. Somebody to drop off." Slipping in the car he closed the door and reversed. The man moved to the side and soundlessly the car moved away. Neither made eye contact.

Lifting his cap, the warden scratched his head. He had specifically returned and waited in the hope of having a long chat, to learn as much as possible about the vehicle. "Drop someone off. He was on his bloody own. Ignorant bugger. Some folk think they're holier than thou!" He continued to grumble whilst heading for the car park opening. "You ask a few polite questions and to some folks it's an intrusion on their bloody liberty." He checked his watch, it was 4.32.

***

Owen looked across the road towards a row of houses before checking the address he had written on the pad. The upstairs curtains were closed. His eyes were drawn to an official sign attached to the wooden railings, the instructions were clear and the block capitals seemed to enforce the statement:

NO TRESPASSING RESIDENTS ONLY WOODFIELD SQUARE.

DC Stuart Park leaned on the steering wheel after reading the sign out loud. "I'm sure the fact that it's by order of HBC will make all the bloody difference."

A blast of a horn from behind startled Park and he glanced in the rear-view mirror. A large wagon heading to the area where a new estate of houses was in the process of construction sat within inches of the rear of the car.

"Where the bloody hell did he come from?" Park started the car and moved away. The wagon's engine was over-revved as if the driver was making a point and moved forward. Finding a parking area, they walked back.

Colin Whiers opened the door. His face flushed red on seeing Owen.

"Have you got something to tell me, Mr Whiers, something you could have told me some time ago. I had another word with Kerry this afternoon. When she sent you a text to say she was worried about Jessica you tried to persuade her to 'leave it', those were the words she used. I think you suggested she should wait and not to act too hastily, that Jessica would turn up. Why did you try to stop her calling the police?"

Whiers opened the door fully and went inside. The two officers followed.

"Who is it, Colin?" A female voice carried down the stairs.

"It's okay, just some old friends." He looked at both men

and offered them a seat. He blushed again. A minute or two later they heard the toilet being flushed.

Owen looked at Park.

"Who is it, Colin?" Owen mimicked the voice.

"A girlfriend and there's no law against it and it's got nothing to do with either of you. Two consenting adults. Now what do you want?" His attitude changed and his whole body tensed.

"What I want is quite simple but first my colleague here is going to caution you as we need to be sure we are being told the truth."

Whiers stood. "I don't need to talk to you. I've cooperated. You can't come here like this."

Both officers stood. "I can arrest you on the evidence we have so far and also whoever is now hiding upstairs and we can all continue this chat at the station. You can leave a note for your mother so she'll know where you are," he paused allowing the threat to sink in, "or we can talk here. Being an adult brings with it certain responsibilities. You can't be a man at night and a little boy in the morning. You, sir, need to make an important decision."

Whiers sat.

"I have it on the best authority that two consenting adults met on the day Sadie Vance went missing. One of those consenting adults was, in fact, Sadie herself and the other ... What were you doing meeting her in the grounds of St John's Church?"

Whiers frowned and shook his head. "Not this soldier."

"I checked with your employer, The Crown Hotel. On that day you were on early shift, breakfast and lunch shift you called it at our last meeting. It's convenient as it gives you a number of opportunities. You can chat or shall we say plot with a colleague who volunteers to come in early," he paused allowing the idea to sink in, "and you also have free time when your girlfriend is working. You know what time does, Colin? We know what the devil makes for people with time on their idle hands. He makes work and not honest work either."

"I've told you I wasn't there." He turned to Park. "You said I didn't have to say anything."

"But it may harm your defence if you do not mention … need I say more?"

Colin Whiers sighed, a psychological white flag. "We were seeing each other, you know. Look, it was sex, that's all."

"Sex, drugs and rock and roll," Park added. "None of the latter? I could make a call and have the drug dog have a sniff around the house while we sit here. Does your mum like dogs going through the place? She keeps a good home we can see that."

As if on cue they heard the front door open and his mother entered the room. She paused and put down the shopping bag she was carrying. "What's going on? Who's this?"

"DI Owen and this is DC Park. Would you be kind enough to bring down whoever is in Colin's bedroom."

She looked at Colin, her face creased demonstrating the anger she felt. "Who's upstairs? I've told you before that my home is not a bloody knocking shop." She turned and within minutes returned. The girl with her was blushing. "Not seen this one before." She pushed her into the room.

Owen realised the situation was getting overcomplicated. He needed to clear the room. Park took the girl and mother to the kitchen. Owen knew she would not talk with Colin in the room.

"Tell me how your meeting with Sadie ended."

"I drove her Vespa, she was pillion. She was a crap rider. I stuck to the side roads as I didn't have a helmet. I left her at the start of Cambridge Terrace. I was meeting Kerry. Sadie just rode off."

"Had she taken any drugs?"

Whiers nodded. "She had a smoke."

"You let her ride the scooter even though she'd taken drugs and she couldn't ride the thing?"

He shrugged his shoulders. "No, I lied. I parked it by a skip. I took the key so she couldn't drive. I might look like a shit but ...

"You supplied it?"

He nodded. "I don't know where she is, that's the truth. She was going to walk home and she was annoyed I wouldn't give her the keys. She kicked the scooter over against the skip, said she hated it and me and she would tell Kerry about the girls. She threw her helmet at me. I couldn't say anything as I was probably the last person to see her. Shit scared I was and then when Jessica went missing, Christ, I'd been with her too the night before at the pub with Kelly. I swear I know nothing about their disappearance."

"So, who's the girl in the kitchen and what did you sell to Sadie?"

Chapter 24

The huge, distinctive white balls marked the skyline at RAF Menwith Hill. Situated close to the A59 on approaching Harrogate they are a well-known landmark. They were clear to see for miles around, as were the many wind turbines positioned a mile or so further along the road. It was here he turned right. The traffic was busy. After a quarter of a mile, he turned left onto Penny Pot Lane, a road that ran for the majority of its length arrow straight. The A59 carried most of the traffic and even in the late afternoon Penny Pot was quiet.

After a mile, hedges filled both sides of the road. They were thick with bushes and trees separating the tarmac from a low, drystone wall that marked the highway boundary. More trees filled the area inland from the wall before giving way to open grassland. Some of the larger trees had fallen, brought down by strong winds, the roots, discs of clogged earth; a natural wattle and daub wall that stood vertical to the now horizontal trunk. There was clearly a justifiable reason why a wind farm had been constructed on this lofty area between the two roads. He pulled onto a dirt track that ran for a short distance at ninety degrees to the road, through the woodland before ending at a metal gate. The heavy leaf cover brought an early darkness with only the sun's long fingers penetrating the lower branches. They elongated myriad shadows before spreading, crooked and deformed in some ways, like fingers and dappling the track's surface and undergrowth. He left the car and walked to one of the fallen trees. The vegetation was thick, brambles clung to his lower legs making walking difficult. That was a good thing, others who dared trespass within this hedgerow wilderness might be easily dissuaded from venturing too far. Even fly-tippers had their limits.

Pausing on the edge of the crater, made as the roots were torn from the ground, he visually assessed the dimensions. It was perfect but so too was the space between the fallen trunk and the ground. Occasionally a car passed at speed. Set within the now darkening late afternoon woodland he would not easily be seen. He returned to the car.

***

Colin Whiers sat facing Owen as Park entered the room. He handed Owen a slip of paper before returning to the kitchen.

"The girl has just told my colleague that she flushed whatever you had down the loo. Classic way if I may say but lacking in imagination. She also tells us that you instructed her to do it if she heard voices in the house. Obviously, you saw me approach. You're in trouble young man, serious trouble. Before I formally arrest you and you accompany me to the station and before we find you legal representation there are two more things. Contact your boss to say you may be with us for some time. You should also let your mother know what you've really been up to. You will then be able to explain to me about Carl Guy and how he found the Vespa."

***

It was the first occasion on which he had deposited a body in the late afternoon, albeit more favourable shadowy light.

Sometimes there's never a perfect time, it's when the opportunity arises, very much like the start of these recent events. It's not all about the planning, there must be some improvisation, some creativity that looks natural and avoids all suspicion. Sadie allowed that, the poor girl, she looked lost and somewhat forlorn. She seemed so unsteady, so vulnerable: a gift and the location were pure chance.

Opening the boot of the car with gloved hands gave clear access to the black cylinder. He threw off the blanket, slid the tube and stood it on end. The corrugated outer skin permitting him to get good purchase; bending his knees allowed the cylinder to fall over his shoulder and with little effort he could haul it level. Care had to be taken moving through the trees as many smaller protruding branches were low and occasionally snagged both the tube and his clothing. On hearing a vehicle approaching he would lower his stance, allowing the front of the tube to rest on the ground but this only occurred twice. If there were no visible movements there would be little chance of being noticed, after all, no one expected to see someone in this place.

Within twenty minutes the entombed Jessica White was positioned directly beneath the horizontal trunk of the fallen tree. It was a perfect fit for a second location, black against black and almost hidden within the tree's shadow. Resting his elbows on the trunk he looked west. The sun skimmed the horizon, the final rays of the day bringing with them the last of the warmth.

"Everything comes to an end, Jessica, from the light comes the dark. It creeps up and catches us all when we least want or expect it to. Strange, I told you before, I liked the dark. It was where I found my peace. I could hide from the noises."

A bird called and the flapping of wings within branches brought a flutter to his own stomach.

"I'll leave you in peace. In some ways, Jessica, I envy you. Good night. Don't let the …"

He did not finish. Collecting a few twigs and branches, he stacked them against the cylinder and the tree trunk to act as temporary camouflage. Standing back, he admired his handiwork before choosing a fresh route through the shrubs and trees to the car. He broke off a lower leafed branch as he went. Closing the boot, he rested the branch by the side of the track and reversed the car towards the edge of the road. There was nothing coming in either direction. Quickly collecting the branch, he brushed both his footprints and car tracks, smudging and eradicating any distinguishable marks. Walking backwards to the car's open door, he continued to sweep away potential evidence before tossing it on to the road side. Once back in the car he removed his shoes; they would be tossed out one at a time at different locations. He laughed thinking how often he had seen shoes on the road or to the road side. Even on motorways he had seen them. Surely each did not represent a missing girl!

***

Park and Owen sat in the interview room. Colin faced them, a copy of his custody record in front of him. His mother's words on leaving the house had clearly had an effect as his attitude since getting in the car and arriving had completely changed. Both being instructed by the custody officer of his rights and seeing the solicitor had compounded the gravity of his situation.

A female officer had escorted the girl home and considering the steady flow of tears she knew the type of reception she would be receiving.

The time had passed quickly as he looked at the solicitor. He had revealed all that he knew and she seemed now to be the only friendly face he had on his side.

"I bumped into Carl as I was heading to meet Kerry. I gave him the key to the scooter. I asked him to ride it and park it near her parents' place, I gave him the address instructing him to push it as close as possible to their drive and leave it. I checked when I walked home to see if he'd moved it. It wasn't there. I only knew she'd not got home when I heard the chatter in the kitchen the following morning. Carl hadn't come in. He just did what I'd asked, he's not a full shilling and he likes to be helpful. I knew that, and in some ways, I abused it, telling him he owed me." He hung his head and a swift series of clicks could be heard as he interlocked his fingers, stretching them backwards.

"Did you drive her from the churchyard back to the town centre? Your words, Mr Whiers, your words."

Whiers frowned and shook his head. "Not exactly."

Chapter 25

He parked the car on the drive and returned the three cement bags to the shed. The garden was bathed in the dying light of a summer's day, the sun had long since dipped over the horizon, leaving the trees a contrasting black against a sky now morphing into a beautiful turquoise before blending into red, orange and yellow. The depth and vibrancy of the colours brought a poem to mind:

'Ensanguining the skies
How heavily it dies
into the west away;
Past touch and sight and sound
Not further to be found,
How hopeless under ground
Falls the remorseful day.'

"Housman, I think if my memory serves me well." He checked the bird table contained food; more was needed but it would have to wait until morning. He began to make his way to the back door. "I need tea," his voice deep and demonstrating the degree of stress he felt. Tea would settle his nerves, it always did. "Then, and only then can I find the courage to check if I've covered my tracks. I can put back the frame beneath the stairs too."

Entering the kitchen, the smell of fried bacon still

lingered.

"You live with this smell throughout your life, Lord Byron, I really must apologise, you being a vegetarian and all – you are a vegetarian, aren't you?" He stared at the hamster as it dug through the potting compost. "I must check, maybe you're not and that would be so remiss of me. You know, I could have dug, buried the evidence like you, but somehow it had to be the tube. Wrapping her in cling film like he did was never acceptable to me, tolerable but it was not the way I would want things to look if they were discovered. If they are found it needs to send a signal. You like being in your tube, I know you do. Now it's time for some tea. Goodness, I've earned it."

After pouring the water from the kettle into the teapot he slipped over the tea cosy. There was, in his opinion, a right and a wrong way to brew tea and a tea bag thrown into a cup was certainly not etiquette.

"There has to be a process, Lord Byron, things have to be done correctly, performed in an orderly fashion to achieve consistency. Tonight, the first night when our friend has left us is always the worst for me. I will think about Jessica out there alone. How many times have we been left alone, ignored and rejected?" He poured the tea into the cup that rested on a saucer. "Out of sight, was out of mind and usually we were left in the dark. Even though she's dead, she's there on her own. At school, if you could call it that, I had a teacher, Jarvis his name, a Mr Jarvis. He taught us about the Egyptians and how they buried their dead in fancy boxes, a sarcophagus, a bit like the cylinders which now hold our friends. They were wrapped too. They weren't alone when they left them, they put all kinds of things in with them for the next life. I didn't like school, but neither did I like home or shall we say they didn't like me. Maybe I should've put Sadie's helmet with her and some chalk and a pebble for Jessica. She could've played hopscotch wherever she ends up." He sipped more tea.

The hamster scurried within the bottom of the cage.

"I don't suppose you worry what happens when the light goes and the world turns to darkness. We never see darkness now, not the darkness I was forced to endure. Even on the darkest of nights there's some light. Moonlight, starlight, streetlight. But real black, the black where you can't see a hand when it's right before your eyes, now that's smothering and it changes you. You realise you're nothing."

***

"Let me give you another scenario, Mr Whiers, let me tell you another story. Remember too that this whole interview is being recorded, what we say and how we respond. It's all on camera. My interpretation of your story, what I believe really happened, however, is backed by some science, Forensic science, a kind of modern-day magic, a magic that baffles the likes of you and me and we just wonder how it's performed. You hope they don't know the difference between truth and lies, fact and what is fiction. Their evidence always tells the truth even when people prefer to hide from that truth. Is that alright with you?"

Whiers turned to his solicitor and nodded whilst shrugging his shoulders in what seemed to be a regular nervous twitch.

"You met her at the churchyard as you said, we can agree on that. She told you she'd managed to get out of going into work by making up a white lie but then she revealed what it was and you didn't find it funny as you had other ideas for the afternoon. It was only after she'd smoked whatever you'd supplied did she tell you she was on her period. She explained she was having a particularly heavy period. Not good, especially there. The next part of the story is key. How did you react?" Owen let the question hang. He was in no hurry, but never took his eyes from Whiers' face. "I'll guess, Mr Whiers, that you weren't too happy, it's not what normally happened, what you expected as you believed you had an agreement. Prostitution of a sort and this wasn't the first occasion. How was she after the smoke, the one you rolled? Not herself, hesitant, giddy, sick maybe or was she just confused and maybe a little paranoid? Did her vomiting put you off, that and the fact she told you about her period? Bloody mess, really!" Owen paused and this time looked at Whiers' legal representative. "Here's where the magic happens. The traces of vomit found near the spot where you were seen has gone for analysis. We have Sadie's DNA and if we add two plus two, we should get four. Your DNA and prints have also been taken as you've been arrested for a recordable offence. We know now your prints were on the scooter and the heart-shaped key ring but we'll get to that."

"So what? It doesn't make me guilty of kidnapping." Whiers sat back with folded arms and stared directly at Owen. It was a false shield of arrogance. Occasionally his facial expression would be his only defence against the comments, a defence that suggested the officer before him was talking bullshit.

"You were angry, so angry you took her scooter keys and left her. You rode back into town on your own. I don't doubt you were seeing your girlfriend that evening. She confirmed it when we asked. You took the backroads to save yourself from being seen. You were unsure as to where to leave the scooter but then you recalled Carl telling you he'd looked in a skip during his morning journey to work, a journey that usually ended in your kitchen. If it were true, it would be so convenient as it was a short walk to the Valley Gardens and Kerry's address.

"When we checked Carl's phone record, more magic, it showed you'd sent him a text at 5.19. He didn't see it as his phone was in his locker. You believed at a certain time Carl would be passing. However, what you didn't know was he'd be late, he'd volunteered to help at the hotel and he hadn't seen your message. You waited behind the skip, yes it was daylight but you sat on the bike, had a vape, maybe, but you were aware that time was passing. You dumped the scooter and then – bang! Serendipity, you saw Carl coming down Parliament Street. You took him to the scooter, found him some rubber workman's gloves from the skip and covered the number plate with the cement bag. Carl isn't that clever to cover his tracks. He didn't want to ride it because of the heart-shaped key ring so you took it off and threw it into the skip. Again, we found it, Colin, as if by magic." Owen tapped the table. From his pocket he withdrew a Forensic bag containing the item and placed it reverently before Whiers. "What puzzles me is how you got him to do these things. That's what I've not worked out but I will. What did you threaten him with? What do you have on him?"

Whiers turned to his solicitor. "Can we talk without him here?"

***

April studied the Forensic evidence she had requested. The remnants of the cardboard tube discovered outside Jessica's apartment showed a strong resemblance to the identified trauma marks on a previous victim. The pathologist had recorded she had received a blow below and just behind the right ear. April found herself pressing the point on herself, it was certainly a sensitive area. The report continued to suggest the attacker might have been aiming for the temple but the actual point of contact was more likely to cause immediate unconsciousness. Knowing whether the attacker struck from the front or rear of the victim would determine their dominant hand but there was no evidence to guide a confirmation or judgement.

Opening the drawer, she removed two different cardboard tubes she had salvaged from the centres of cling film and kitchen foil rolls. Both fit her hand perfectly. One was thirty-four centimetres long, the other thirty; both had an identical diameter of two and a half centimetres. Apart from the size there was a difference in colour. The evidence suggested that the weapon used was unbleached, brown in colour. She concentrated on that one. Holding the tube as one would hold a dagger, she felt that an effective strike could be made using a horizontal, sweeping blow away from her own body. Placing the tube in the opposite way, the blow would sweep in front of her. It was this move that seemed to her more controlled, more accurate in order to hit a specific spot. She tapped the tube on the desk before collecting her phone and checking her contact list.

***

On their return to the interview room Owen could

immediately sense a change in not only Whiers' attitude, but also in that of his solicitor who gave Owen a slight nod before taking his seat.

The solicitor spoke and Whiers remained silent. "Mr Whiers offers this written statement of facts, detailing the meeting between himself and Sadie Vance as a true record of what went on that afternoon." She slid the handwritten notes across the table. It was Owen's turn to frown. He read them out loud. On conclusion he looked at the two signatures on the concluding page.

"You blackmailed Carl? Gave him a smoke and told him he'd smoked drugs in the hotel but it wasn't, it was tobacco. You threatened he'd lose his job if he didn't ..." Owen shook his head. He watched as tears began to stream down Whiers' cheeks. Initially there was no sound but then he spoke, an explosion of words.

"I was shit scared when I heard she'd gone missing, I didn't know what to think or do. I'd heard of people dying from choking on their own vomit but she hadn't been found anywhere. My mind closed down. Kerry knew there was something wrong. When we were at The Winter Gardens later and Jessica came in and they started talking about her I just had to leave, made an excuse about mum having a problem. You'll not believe this but I'm glad it's out in the open, the truth that is. All I can say is I'm sorry!"

***

April had worked with Pete Dulson early on in her career. He had become a police firearms officer after an exemplary military career. He was retired but taught self-defence and unarmed combat to various groups. She knew that he had achieved black belts in two forms of karate.

"If anyone can help it's you, Pete. A cardboard tube as a weapon. What can you tell me?"

"Very plausible, as is a rolled-up newspaper, both innocent in their own right to anyone seeing them carried or finding them near the scene of an attack. They look like litter, everyday street detritus. I need to show you how and what. Skype me. Good job I'm decent, Richmond!"

Pete Dulson had positioned his phone enabling the camera to give a clear view of the room. He appeared with a nunchaku, a martial arts weapon comprising what looked like two short broomstick handles connected by a short chain.

"I couldn't find a cardboard tube but this will give you the idea. A stout tube as you've described could cause serious injury depending on the expertise of the user and the strength and position of the strike." He held the end of the wood with both hands covering the lower end of the stick. "By removing the lower hand your tube is now in the perfect position, there's a short part protruding from my fist. Consider this now to be the head of a hammer. I can strike with it and because it's short, I have perfect control."

He demonstrated a number of strikes.

"The opposite section you can think of as a knife, or a dagger. This would be for striking upwards to the groin, beneath the chin, sideways to the kidney area or even to the bridge of the nose but that would be very messy. You have less control in this position but for striking a greater target area it can be truly effective. So, the short part of your tube is the hammer, the longer, the knife or dagger. Two weapons in one just by positioning the hand correctly."

"The victim was struck here." She demonstrated. "A

young female."

"A back hand hammer blow would see an immediate result, unconsciousness, even severe internal damage depending on the accuracy of the blow. If the person was proficient, April, they'd only need one strike."

April picked up the tube and positioned her hand as he had demonstrated to her.

"Perfect. Now swing sideways horizontally. The force is concentrated on such a tiny spot. Even a blow to the temple or cheek would cause damage but if you wanted someone quickly out for the count, that's the way to do it. Afterwards, you put the tube in the recycling or a stream or river and it breaks down naturally."

April hung up and looked at the tube. Knowing the technique made the possibility real. Moving to the white board she wrote key notes.

***

Owen left the defendant with the custody officer and it would be in the hands of the PPS as to whether he would remain in custody or be released on bail. Whiers had intimidated a witness in the past and he was unsure if bail would be granted.

Chapter 26

The day was hot, Cyril pushed the pram towards the rocket-like spire of St Mary's Church, Studley Royal, that stood at the end of the narrow strip of tarmac and was nestled within the sweeping grounds of the deer park. Julie walked by his side, her arm linking his. They paused and looked down the track in the opposite direction, the twin towers of Ripon Cathedral, way in the distance, shimmered in the early afternoon heat. The separation of the two religious houses for some reason made him think of Owen.

"Owen will be like a cat on hot bricks. He'll be watching me to make sure I'm neither pushing his boy too quickly nor too slowly, checking whether Christopher is in shade from the sun, wondering if he's awake or asleep, hungry or thirsty."

"He's a protective and proud father and he has every right to know how you drive." She tugged his arm playfully. "He did laugh as he watched you struggle getting the travel cot secured onto the seat of the old Bentley."

Cyril pulled a face suggesting innocence. "It was my first time! Anyway, old cars were not designed for this newfangled, transformer-type maternity equipment. I managed in the end."

"Since when were you familiar with the oldfangled

stuff?" She did not give him time to protest. "Succeed you did, my love, I was proud of you but I must say I've carried out quicker autopsies. To make matters worse, I thought he was going to have kittens when you narrowly missed that group of cyclists and had to brake hard."

"Middle of the road and on the wrong bloody side. Think they own the place. I shouldn't have come. I could have gone to the pub if all you want is a whipping boy for the afternoon."

"Don't sulk, Bennett, it brings out the worst in you." She leaned forward and kissed his cheek. "I bet the missing women, girls really when you consider their ages at nineteen and twenty-two, have brought the responsibility of parenting into sharp focus for both of them. He's probably played a number of mental scenarios putting this little fella in their place."

"I've noticed. There's a fire within him, a determination, maybe it's an anger ... I saw it when I was watching the video link of his interview with one of the suspects. I see it in the team." He paused momentarily and looked at the church. "They're working so closely together, it's more like a family. I have to say I'm so impressed with April, not only because she's established herself as the keystone but for her generosity of spirit. She's kind, Julie, firm but kind. My only fear is she'll be gone soon. I knew when she came it was a fast-track appointment."

"She is who she is as a copper because of you. You're a generous boss, you give her the freedom to act on her own initiative just as you have guided Owen. Goodness, if you think how he was when we first knew him!" She squeezed his arm and it brought a smile to Cyril's face.

"I seem to drive my desk more and more and I miss the practical side a lot but knowing the team is behind me fills me with confidence and a different kind of job satisfaction. It's a complex case, a challenge and that is what keeps me in the job."

"You'll need to watch him, Cyril. He might be a gentle giant but he has a different perspective on these things now. You feel he's frustrated at the slow progress, don't you?"

"Yes, probably. Usually, cases like this solve themselves or the missing person is swiftly found but the longer the case goes on and the evidence grows more sparse – the less likely we'll see a positive outcome. You know what that means and so does Owen. Anyway, that's shop talk and you're here to do the following, pick on me, rest, relax and enjoy a lovely picnic. That's why they're called just that … pick …" He didn't finish the sentence but chuckled at his own joke.

Julie stopped and looked across at the folding grasslands that stretched far away. Within the shade of the tree a herd of deer grazed. Nothing could be further away from the human heartache they both witnessed on a daily basis.

"We should come here more often, Cyril. It helps restore faith in today's world."

"He's not been able to settle since you two went off," Hannah announced as she sat in a comfortable-looking picnic chair whilst Owen leaned against a tree. "If I heard the words, 'they've been a long time' once I heard it ten times. I thought I'd have to nail him to that tree to stop him coming looking."

Owen flushed bright red as he lifted Christopher from the pram but said nothing in his defence.

"Is my no claims bonus still intact, Owen? Hopefully, I'll get to push the little fella again." Cyril winked at Hannah, cleaned his hands with a wet wipe before leaning over and removing a piece of pork pie from the Tupperware tub. "Appleton's?"

Julie nodded and poured herself a glass of wine. "Come, Hannah, you've been sitting long enough. Let's stroll and leave the men holding the baby."

Hannah stood, collected her glass of water and walked across the grass.

"I know it's not easy, I can tell even though I have never had children. I'm still a doctor. You know you can come to me whenever you need. Leave Christopher for a day or two if you need a complete break."

"Can I leave Owen, too?" There was a pause and then she giggled. "I'm kidding, but that's good to know. My head's all over the place and I'm so exhausted. I never seem to catch up and yet I'd give anything for a couple of days back with you. Is that wrong of me?"

"No, you're so good at your job, a job that gave you so much satisfaction it's understandable. It will be there when you are ready but do enjoy the time you have now, it will never return, they grow and develop only once and so quickly. I look at Owen and see a different man, Hannah. What you too have is so special but I know you may look on all the blessings, the baby, a loving partner and a new home but feel it's not enough. Many women have what's called baby blues but that's a few weeks after the birth. I'll pop round once a week and we can take Christopher out.

The home can seem so claustrophobic and the child demanding. Trust me, Hannah, I'm a doctor."

They both laughed as they approached the expanse of water below the waterfall. The noise of children feeding the ducks seemed to lighten the mood.

"It won't be long before you'll be following after him whilst he chases the ducks."

"Thank you, Julie. You don't know how much I needed this chat. Let's get back. I think I might have found some of my appetite."

***

April walked Ralph down the path that led from Coppice Drive along Luchon Way. The trees seemed to protect what appeared to be a natural, shallow valley, a green way trapped within the urban setting. She paused to enjoy the bird song whilst Ralph took the moment to scratch behind his ear, a contortion that seemed both physically impossible and uncomfortable. "If our attacker struck using a tube as Pete has suggested, then that would be quiet, if accurate there would be little sound. The body striking the floor would incur injuries and yet none was identified on a previous possible victim. So, Ralph, what did he or she do?"

Ralph, hearing his name stopped and turned to look at her.

The child's play area was busy. Hampsthwaite Road was to her left just beyond the rise in the grass. Reducing the length of Ralph's lead, she crossed the grassland. In the distance sat Jessica's apartment building. When interviewed, the neighbour had mentioned that Jessica could have returned along Luchon Way but she had also added the caveat, that it would not be a route for a lone female to take at dusk. She was probably correct. The area had been checked but they had not done a full sweep.

On approaching the front of the building, her eyes were first drawn to a short piece of blue and white police tape dangling from one of the shrubs set in the garden to the front. Her focus was soon redirected to the hopscotch squares. It brought her to a sudden stop and made her heart sink. They looked to have faded with the previous morning's rain, an act of remorse like wiping the slate clean of any involvement. Just looking at it made the hairs on her neck rise and she shivered.

The door to the apartment block opened and a couple emerged. They looked at the dog and then at her.

"Can we help?"

April smiled. "No, seeing that just took me back to my childhood." She knew it would be the opportunity they might need to talk. She started to mentally count 1, 2, 3 …

"Have you not heard about the girl who's gone missing? Second one too. It's been in the news and the police have posted notes locally asking for information. It's also on their website. Lovely dog."

"Thanks, his name's Ralph. Did you see her much, know her, the missing girl?"

"Saw her go jogging now and again but we didn't know her. Knew her name, Jessica but that's all. I remember a bloke she had visit. He stayed regularly but we've not seen him for a while. We heard a few things that went on from those living closer to her apartment: rows, arguments and the odd slamming door and they weren't even married!" He laughed but his partner nudged him. "Sorry, not very respectful."

"I'm surprised nobody saw or heard anything the night she went missing. If it had been my place …" April nonchalantly stroked Ralph's ears.

She noticed them look at each other and then turn back. There was a reluctance in their answer. "It's probably something and nothing, false gossip, but a mate of mine says he was walking past and he saw a couple in a romantic clinch but then he also witnessed the hit and run at the station. Any disaster he's seen it. Like's the booze a little too much. Bit of a Walter Mitty he is."

She wondered if they knew Mr Mitty never existed, being a fictitious character created for a short story.

"I suppose he's one of those who's forever at the police station."

"Nope, I told him he should say something what with the appeals but then you don't know his missus, if she knew he been out at that time. She works late, a waitress, I think at a restaurant in town. They have an agreement, they share the care, he says. His mother lives with them, she has Alzheimer's. I often see him nipping for a last one."

"Do you live here?"

"Yes, for all I've had to say it's normally really peaceful. Number 4."

April smiled. "Let's hope she's found safe and well." She raised her hand and walked down the slope with the words, *romantic embrace* flooding her thoughts. She needed to call the office.

Chapter 27

Monday always seemed to present its own difficulties but it was never a problem resuming the handover meeting of the investigation and to April this was critical, it meant not only a break, but different eyes working with the evidence received. She knew that she never switched off, never let it go. "Close the bloody hangar door," people had advised her, but she could not do it, she never could and that was probably the reason she failed to maintain a relationship for any length of time. It was always somewhere in her mind, revising and reviewing the minutiae. If there were a consolation, it was what, she believed, made her a good copper. The call she had made to control on returning from the walk had been acted upon and proved to be fruitful; she had a name and a contact number. However, she knew that it needed sensitive handling. Getting witness statements was about trust, sensitivity and a bit of give and take. She wanted to deal with this in her own way. She needed Cyril's advice too.

Unusually, Julie had dropped Cyril at the front door of the station. The morning summer shower and the need to carry a large jar of sweets provided the incentive to forego the usual walk. He deposited the jar on Owen's desk before moving through to his office. Although the initial part of the morning ritual had changed, Cyril was still a creature of habit; the jacket was popped onto the hanger, the desk was swiftly ordered, each item being moved into its exact place; he was sure the cleaning staff enjoyed disturbing things just to prove they'd done their job. Once everything was in order, it would be tea. Picking up the small bronze statuette of Moses, a wedding gift from the team, he studied the fine detail and the signature.

"Thou shalt not kill." April's words came softly and he turned, startled by the intrusion. "One of the ten." She held up the cardboard tube. "May I have a word?"

He stood, grunted a form of greeting before pointing to the chair set to the front of his desk.

"I spoke with a friend earlier today who's an expert in his field. This tube can have the same effect as a hammer or knife blow if used correctly." She demonstrated quickly by gripping the tube before recapping the findings she had unearthed regarding the damage sustained by a previous kidnap victim. "Evidence points to something like this being used to incapacitate but we both know that. I believe strongly that Jessica was abducted from the front of her apartment and I have clear evidence ..." She waved the tube but now held it as she had when Pete had demonstrated its possible use as a weapon. "I believe this to be the weapon of choice. By this afternoon I should have a clear understanding and further proof, but initially, I'd like to put my theory to the test with your help."

Cyril rested his elbows on the desk, interlocked his fingers and placed them beneath his chin. "The stage is yours, April, do your worst."

"No, sir, I need you, you are involved in the

demonstration. I'll take the place of Jessica, you, the kidnapper. The evidence suggests that one of the previous victims we discussed at the briefing, never hit the ground after being struck at this spot here." She turned her head to the side and pointed out the location as she spoke. "This would have caused her to black out and collapse. I need to talk to Julie at some point about that or maybe you can get a definitive answer. Remember, according to the pathologist's report, she exhibited no other injuries just the damage to the side of her head. It's my belief the attacker knew exactly what he was doing and after striking hard he was ready to catch her. You'll note that the two latest kidnap victims are similar in height, size and weight, they're light, around the fifty some kilograms. With the car boot open it's a case of bang, catch and in. How long would that take?"

"You're suggesting what exactly?"

"You stand near to me, let's say a metre away and using this tube as if it's in the hammer position, you strike like this. As soon as you gently touch me, I'll collapse and your task is to catch me before I hit the floor. I'm relying on you! According to my expert, the strike should be one sweeping horizontal motion to ensure maximum force like this." She demonstrated on an imaginary figure. "Before we do this there's the issue of the tube." She handed Cyril the weapon.

He followed the same run through as she had demonstrated. "The tube will get in the way of the catching process as it protrudes too far."

She smiled. "Bingo! My thoughts exactly and so?"

"Strike and throw?"

"You read my mind. It would hit the floor with some force and I believe that's why SOCO found the card residue containing blood, hair and skin cells. If we can prove that the strike and catch is feasible, I'll leave here happy."

They only needed the one attempt. The strike was gentle but Cyril threw the tube with force as he saw April collapse for real. He thrust his arms under hers keeping her upright, her face just to the side of his. At this point neither knew Owen was at the door holding the jar of Uncle Joe's mints.

He cleared his throat. "Is this what you meant by a Damascene moment, April Richmond? My eyes have been well and truly opened."

Both turned as they separated. April straightened her clothing, "You could say it's a seminal moment, Owen." A touch of anger laced her words. "Give the big man a little knowledge and he'll try to make you look a fool!"

"Sorry, I meant it as a joke. Awkward! Mint anyone?"

April shook her head. "I'll keep you posted, sir. If you want to explain to our misguided colleague here what we were trying to achieve, be my guest. By the way, the force of your throw demonstrated the tube would leave residue on striking a hard, irregular surface. That's what they found at the scene."

"Right. I'd really no choice, your fall was so fast. It was either hold the tube and you'd fall or ..."

April left with a skip in her step.

Owen frowned. "You've made a lady very happy, sir. That was all very dramatic. Do you think I should apologise to April?" He dropped some mints onto the desk.

"No, Owen, it was called friendly banter. She'll get over

it."

As Owen left Cyril phoned Julie. It went to answerphone. He checked his watch, collected his keys and left his office.

Cyril always felt welcomed by the receptionist as he was directed towards Julie's office, directions he did not need but politely accepted. He paused outside the door and admired the name plate. It brought a flush of pride. He only needed the slightest excuse to call.

"Come in, Cyril!" The voice seemed to echo in the corridor.

Leaning round he grinned. "My favourite pathologist."

"You have exactly twelve minutes before I have to leave. You can then stay but you must promise not to play with the specimen jars, especially your favourite." She looked towards the jar on the lower shelf. Cyril blushed slightly. She grinned, enjoying the moment.

Cyril explained April's theory and received a brief but definitive answer. Julie stood and collected the items from her desk.

"A sharp blow can be quite devastating depending on the individual and a stout tube would do the trick."

Cyril removed his mobile. "I need to make a call."

"Close the door when you leave." She blew him a kiss.

The number was engaged. He stood and moved towards the lower shelf whilst glancing at the door. Taking hold of the specimen jar, he held it to the light as the office door opened. It was Julie. Cyril swiftly moved the jar behind his back, a startled look on his face.

"We women are always right. Male inferiority, Cyril, a common trait. Now put it back!" She forced back the smile.

"In flagrante delicto, my man. You have work to do and so have I. Come!"

***

Geoffrey Conroy was nothing like what April had expected. She had the impression of a timid and demure individual, afraid of his own shadow let alone his spouse. How different her initial perception proved to be.

"DI Richmond?" He smiled and thrust a hand towards her. "Do come in."

The ground floor apartment was orderly. Polished oak furniture seemed to fill the space complimented by a floral two piece suite. She noticed a small mouse carved to the leg of one of the side tables. A number of what appeared to be military plaques were positioned next to group photographs, carefully positioned around the walls.

He smiled. "Military career. Different parts of the world. Miss it terribly. Do sit." The short sharp sentences came over as orders. She sat. "My wife's out as you know. My mother's asleep. She tends to have difficulty sleeping through the night, often wanders, confuses different rooms believing it's the toilet. Frightfully sad. However, the consolation is she sleeps well about this time, until lunch then we start again. Dreadful illness. If she were a dog ..." Noticing April's expression, he failed to finish the sentence.

Conroy stood over six feet tall, he was broad at the shoulders and immaculately dressed. The apartment was warm but he still wore a sweater, shirt and tie. His beige trousers were perfectly pressed and even his slippers seemed polished.

"Thank you for seeing me, I know it can be difficult. I believe your wife works in a restaurant?"

"Work, yes, but she's a partner in the business hence the time it takes. She's a partner with her brother. She's Greek Cypriot, that's where we met, Cyprus. Good business too but so time-consuming. I'm retired and my mother needs support. We'd only just downsized in preparation for a life of travel but then … My advice to you, young lady, is to make your dreams a reality whilst you still can as tomorrow might be too late." He frowned. "Sorry, I'm instructing and not conversing. Bad habit. How may I help?"

April talked him through the outline of the case.

"I did see something but it was neither sinister nor out of place. I'd nipped for a nightcap, breath of fresh air also. Being here all day can be very claustrophobic. Anyway, as I walked down Hampsthwaite Road I noticed a couple. There are two entrances to that block of apartments and both are for pedestrians and cars as you probably know, but the rest of the façade is blocked from view by shrubbery."

"The couple?" April was eager for more specifics.

"Yes, sorry. They were standing apart when I first saw them but then she seemed to fling herself at him or maybe it was the other way round. Either way they ended up in an embrace. Naturally I looked away at that point."

"Was there a car?"

"Yes, a dark colour. Come to think about it I believe the tailgate …" he demonstrated with his hands, "… was open. I've just remembered that. Maybe the grey cells aren't as bad as I think they are."

"Did you look again?"

"No, but the car passed me when I was nearer home."

"Did you notice anything about it?"

"There was only one person in it and it was dark in

colour, either electric or hybrid. It was almost silent, just whined a tad as they do. Unreal if you ask me, they creep up on you. Driving slowly too. Probably heading for the A61."

"Why did he not turn left immediately from the flats?"

Conroy just looked at April. "If I were to answer that question it would have to be a guess and I suspect, Detective Inspector, you're here for facts and not what I think happened. If you go the way the car was travelling, in my opinion it's because you can get onto the A61 at the traffic lights. It's safer. They do that at busy times if they want to head out of town. But at that time of the evening, there would be few traffic issues. That's opinion and not fact." He folded his arms as if to signal he knew no more.

April finished, adding the final comments to the statement on the electronic pad before handing it to Conroy. "If you'd just read through that and if it's correct add your signature, I'll leave you in peace."

Taking his glasses from on top of the newspaper beside him he read through it. "Does one correct the punctuation or …?" he looked over the glasses and then winked. "Kidding. There you go. I must apologise for not thinking this important. There was nothing suspicious. I shouldn't leave mother alone, bad show on my behalf but sometimes one needs sensible company and conversation. There's only so many crosswords a man can do." He escorted her to the door.

The fresh air hit her as she walked to the car. Leaning on the roof she took a huge lungful. Her phone rang, it was Owen.

"We've found a body. Kex Gill on the A59. Road traffic

accident has brought it to light. A car struck the barrier and the caravan it was towing flipped over. A witness following behind suggested it may have been clipped by an artic climbing the hill. From what they say, the body's in a bloody plastic tube but it's way down in the gill. I'm also informed it's what's known as a twinwall drain pipe. We believe it may be Sadie Vance. The doctor has arrived but as yet is not with the body. The road's been closed as it was necessary to get the air ambulance in for the car driver. SOCO are on their way too. Fate, April, without the accident, I doubt we'd have found it."

"Bloody hell!" She thumped the roof of the car and then paused. It dawned on her that finding one body would mean that they would now be looking for a second. "A tube, Owen, like a pipe? Is it in the ground?" She immediately thought of the exercise she had performed with Cyril early in the day.

"No, it was just sitting in the valley bottom as if it's been rolled there from the road."

"Is Flash with you?" The wind up on the moor appeared stronger as the phone amplified the sound and distorted Owen's voice. Flash had been the nickname given to Cyril Bennett early in his police career, not because of his immaculate dress sense but his name being linked to Gordon Bennett, the philanthropist and then for reasons lost in the smog of time to Flash Gordon. The sobriquet, Flash stayed but few dared use it to his face.

"Yes, we're at the site where the car mounted the barrier. There's little left of the caravan. The emergency team checking the site stumbled across the pipe down in the gill. I'll talk more when I get down there if I can get a signal. We'll need family support at Sadie Vance's house before any news of the discovery of a body is made public, you know how news travels."

April dropped the phone onto the car roof. Although she had anticipated this might be the outcome after the length of time since Sadie had gone missing, it still hit her hard. Collecting her phone, she made the request call to organise professional help for the family.

Chapter 28

The A59 had been closed at Blubberhouses, police vehicles straddled the road and traffic heading towards Skipton from the Harrogate area was now diverted via a circuitous route towards Otley. April could only imagine the immediate aftermath of the accident and the repercussions it would have on the traffic in general. It was a busy road on most days and was not built for the size of many of the vehicles using the route. It was a road more suited to the traffic of the 1930s than that of today. She had often travelled it and on many occasions imagined mail coaches being hauled along by a team of horses and she felt sure it had not changed that much over the years. It was a moment's distraction before she Googled, 'twinwall pipe'.

Owen stood with Cyril. Both now wore light blue protective coveralls. They stood just above the spot where the car had made contact with the crash barrier. The boot area of the vehicle sat high on the steel Armco but was still attached to the chassis. The remnants of the caravan were now a distorted and twisted skeleton positioned like a modern latticed sculpture.

"Bloody hell, it must have turned to matchwood in seconds from the look of it. I've seen more robust houses made of cards!"

Cyril climbed onto the wall and peered into the valley. There were a few suited figures from the first SOCO unit to arrive. After erecting the Forensic tent, they had moved away from the immediate location until further equipment had been brought down. It was key strategy to preserve whatever Forensic evidence might remain. The pathologist, Cyril was informed, was already at the scene. He knew it would be Caner.

The terrain was steep and fell away towards a number of mature trees, each blown by the prevailing wind that had been channelled through the valley over the years. It had formed and moulded their blasted shape, in some ways giving them a prematurely aged and almost primeval appearance.

Police vehicles lined the road, the flash of the blue strobe lights overpowered the sunlight and remained visible. Cyril informed Owen he was going to take a closer look as he moved towards the far edge of the wall. He jumped the metre and a half to land close to the far side of the stonework but then the rest of the route towards the beck was mainly executed out of his control and on his backside. Owen nearly wet himself and moved away from the wall not wanting to be seen or to watch the finale of his superior's undignified slide. Fortunately, the light blue coverall had taken the brunt of the journey by collecting the green skid stains rubbed from the grass and bracken. To those watching below, it had brought a degree of mirth to a tragic scene. He had not been the first to arrive in such an undignified manner but even so, he felt greatly embarrassed.

On getting to his feet, Cyril was pleased to observe the

main crime scene had been secured with a second row of police tape. An officer manned the only designated entry and exit point.

Cyril could only speculate as to what had been discovered but the description from first responders left little to the imagination. He had been told that the cylinder lay partly in the shallow beck with the uppermost end nestled against a broken sapling and it had remained intact. Initially, they had believed it to be a piece of piping left over from the ground works but on closer inspection, as they had broken open one of the endcaps, the grisly truth had been revealed. They had discovered the body, presumed to be that of Sadie Vance. Their description was vivid. As luck would have it, Cyril was positioned upwind and grateful that it would allow any potential stench from the decomposing flesh to drift away from him.

Within fifteen minutes after entering, Caner emerged from the Forensic tent and placed his feet on the step plates before ducking beneath the tape. He deposited his gloves in a yellow hazard bag attached to a metal spike that held part of the police tape. Dropping his mask below his chin, he then pulled back his hood. Cyril saw him gulp in air.

Owen, who had come down escorting two members of the SOCO team from higher up the valley, joined Cyril and watched Caner's approach.

"It wasn't a Visitation from God, that I can safely say, Cyril. Trapped in that tube there's been rapid decomposition. Like a greenhouse. The black surface has certainly been a conduit for the sun's heat, made a perfect environment for …" He did not finish his sentence as the words seemed unnecessary considering the condition and location of the corpse. "Female, young, but owing to the constriction within the pipe, I cannot make a proper diagnosis of time of death other than to confirm she is dead. I've used an endoscope and I can safely say the woman died once placed within it, she was not entombed post-mortem. She also didn't enter of her own accord as her hands and feet are bound. She's positioned like a diver, Cyril, I can see your brain working overtime. We'll need to get the whole thing back to the mortuary, once we have the Coroner's consent, of course. I can't work here effectively enough and I need to extract the body without damaging the evidence. One of the unpleasant ones I'm afraid to report."

Cyril could see the puzzlement on Owen's face. "Visitation?"

"What you might find on a Victorian death certificate, Owen, 'Visitation from God' or 'Heaven' meaning they died of natural causes. The statement covered all kinds of unknowns. Science and medicine have allowed us to move on thank the Lord."

"Right! It has a certain ring to it, somehow a gentle way to say he or she has kicked the old bucket. To tell someone their father's cause of death was a Visitation from God sounds better than a bloody heart attack."

Cyril said nothing as he watched the SOCO continue their work in securing the site and extracting evidence.

Caner's phone rang. Cyril paused and waited.

"We now have permission to move the body as is. Unusually swift response, I know but the terrain is difficult and it needs moving as soon as. I informed him I have all the evidence I can collect here at present."

Guided by Cyril and Caner, Owen walked back up the less steep slope that led to a gate on the side of the A59. For Cyril it looked far more difficult than his earlier arrival.

"Will you be attending the autopsy, Cyril?" Caner was moving towards his car as he spoke.

"Owen finds them more fascinating and I'm a generous boss, so no."

Caner had already anticipated his answer.

"Strange bloke, Caner. I always feel he looks down on the lower ranks," Owen muttered.

"As you're a clear six inches taller, Owen, I doubt that. He's just old school."

Cyril turned to observe the crime scene. "The cylinder was obviously launched from the wall about there and allowed to roll. The inner weight would've ensured enough momentum to carry it to the bottom no matter how thick the bracken." He turned and stared at the ruin of the building to the right of the road, the track, built when the road was repaired, was also taped off and two scene of crime officers were working the area.

"Emergency services have called the Upper Wharfdale Fell Mountain Rescue Team to aid in the removal of the cylinder so that should be out soon. My assumption is they'll keep it within the pipe until they perform the autopsy."

Looking towards the track, Owen stood and took a few photographs. "The short slip road leading to that gate and the ruin is the only way it could have arrived here, the only parking space. It wasn't carried and they couldn't park on the road no matter what time of day it was done."

"Is that the reason for the cylinder, Owen, to enable it to roll and hopefully be lost down here? Was it chosen deliberately as a way of transporting the body to areas that don't see regular footfall?"

"Maybe, but a roll, a tube in this case, is the easiest way to move a dead weight. Carpets and rugs were a favourite method in the old films. You can stand them on their end and let them fall over your shoulder. The rigidity is the key. It also hides the body during transportation. Get it to that wall and the barrier, lay it flat and just give it a shove and voilà, it disappears at an increasing speed and considering this location has an indeterminate stay. Magic!"

"Voilà!" Cyril raised an eyebrow. "Right Owen. There was no magic, my friend. This location was planned for the very reasons you so professionally described."

Cyril noticed the photographer from the local press standing high on the bank on the opposite side of the road to the incident. The camera lens, as long as his forearm, was focused on the busy scene below. Cyril removed his phone but there was no signal. He raised his voice and pointed to two officers and then in the direction of the journalist. The officers responded immediately by scrambling towards the reporter.

"Bloody press!" Cyril grumbled as he pulled off the coverall. "I want to see what he's got on that camera." His voice carried. One of the officers approaching the cameraman raised his hand in the air in response.

"You've always advised me to treat the press as an ally, a useful tool. What if he's got photographs of the cylinder?"

Cyril shrugged. "The key is to minimise journalistic speculation, that way we kill two birds with one stone, Owen, we minimise the anxiety amongst the public and unashamedly promote the force. Here endeth the lesson.

Where was I? April! April thinks her victim was attacked using a cardboard tube, a cylinder. Then we find your victim was stashed in one. Now what do you make of that, Owen?"

"Coincidence. Let's wait for the autopsy."

Owen approached the cameraman, checked his ID and looked at the photographs taken before reaching a professional understanding. Both knew there was a need for co-operation.

Unusually, Owen drove. The traffic snaked back along Hopper Lane and Skipton Road but at least it was moving only dissipating as Menwith Hill came into view. Cyril kept the blue strobes on to facilitate a faster return.

"April thinks her missing girl will be found dead now, she believes it's inevitable. I can sense it. When I spoke to her an hour or so back it was obvious in her voice. The worry is, if he's taken two, will there be a third?" Owen watched the road.

"Get in touch with our news desk. I need to prepare a report for a general appeal, press and media enquiries. I also want to be seen to help our co-operative cameraman, that's how we work with allies, Owen. It doesn't take long for these things to hit the Internet. I believe permitted police pictures of the accident have already been posted. I also want to issue a public statement and I want it done today."

Owen slipped his phone from his pocket and made the arrangements.

***

April had printed images of the twinwall pipe and added them to the Incident Room wall. She had located suppliers and distributors. The exact make and specification would soon be established and a more in-depth search could be carried out. She had also requested checks using the computer records detailing stolen items as apparently over the last twelve months there has been several recorded thefts of similar pipes. The locations of the thefts were added to the UK map she had created earlier.

Shakti entered and April explained the significance of the new markings.

"You'll only have a record for large thefts," Shakti surmised. "Building sites lose loads of odds and sods, not only through the one or two going missing but there's handling damage and natural wastage. Remember too that they've just finished work on the A1M junction for Harrogate and they used stacks of similar pipes. Damaged ones are probably tossed to one side or 'given' to workers." She threw her hands out as if to suggest the figures were plausible but not necessarily accurate. "They're accounted for in a sense but some are probably still out there, if you get my meaning. The odd construction worker picked one or two surplus ones and made some spare pocket change. Those, April, will never be tracked – they'll be the ones our perpetrator would use. If it were me, I would. There's so much building work going on around Harrogate and district there must be a fair few knocking about. Maybe our man is in that very trade!"

"Or woman. Thanks for that Shak. I love it when you interact with me. I seem to take one step forward and then two back." They both laughed.

"Once you have the name of the pipe manufacturer you'll be in a stronger position."

***

Owen and Cyril came into the Incident Room. Those working stopped and listened as Cyril gave a brief summary of events. "The Media Manager is due here," he checked his watch, shook it and looked again, "in ten minutes and will be briefing us on the requests coming in for information from our press friends and to prepare copy for the statements we will be posting. I'll talk you through what I feel is required at this stage. We've all done it before but it has to be right. It's a sensitive process as you all know so feel free to contribute at any time, nothing is off the agenda. So, we need information from members of the public who travelled along the A49 through Kex Gill. I'm aware that many will be unfamiliar with that exact location so make sure it clearly identifies the road linking Harrogate and Skipton between the dates Sadie Vance went missing and today. Photographs, aerial shots maybe linked to some kind of map might help. Now for the car?" He turned to April.

"A dark coloured estate. We believe it to be either electric or hybrid. We have nothing yet from ANPR or CCTV."

"Thanks, April. We require the public to come forward if they remember seeing this type of vehicle parked near the area. We're also looking for anyone seen moving or transporting a section of plastic pipe but that will be on a separate information request. I don't want speculative links to the finding of the body and the pipe if it can be avoided."

Nixon stood and appeared from behind one of the many computer screens. "Here are some facts regarding the type of car we're looking for just within our area, that's dark coloured, hybrid and electric vehicles registered in North Yorkshire, which does surprise me as Harrogate was revealed to be one of the worst areas prepared for the electric vehicle revolution."

His figures brought some gasps and a few expletives with the growing chatter in the room.

"It gets worse." The screen changed. "Four hundred and seventy thousand electric cars have been registered to date within the UK and from just what I've seen on the road, many of those vehicles are dark colours. Initially, when they were made there seemed to be a limited colour choice. This type of car tends to be bloody expensive too, and from speaking to a friend in the car trade there's a high turnover in the second-hand market. All to do with owners having battery paranoia. No one wants to risk being the one to collect the eye-watering bill when it comes to needing a new battery. My point is, the owners will have a reasonable income. We could search DVLA using driver demographics but that wouldn't take into account business vehicles or rentals. As for hybrids? Most new vehicles have some kind of hybrid system so thankfully ordering a search in that area isn't my call."

"What does that type of car tell us about an owner, other than the cost of ownership?" Cyril queried. "Start in the Harrogate areas, between here and Skipton. Let's not forget this person has to carry not only the girl's weight within the tube but they also have to have the ability to manoeuvre a dead weight into the car and out of it. Whoever put her in the pipe didn't do it in the back of an estate car. Another question, are we looking for either sex? What age might they be? They're all questions we must consider but also be prepared for a curved ball."

"I know some fit seventy-year-olds and some powerful

women …" Owen stopped and frowned before spreading his arms. "How long's a piece of string? I don't think age matters, it's fitness and strength."

The Incident Manager popped her head round the door. "Sad news. We've had calls already about the accident and also speculation considering the CSIs being present. Bees to the honeypot."

***

"Murphy's Law, Lord Byron. If anything can go wrong it will! It looks like it has. You can never fully plan these things. I've said it before, no matter what you do there's always a chance Murphy will come along and cock it up. Bad accident too from the police Facebook page. Air ambulance went in but goodness knows where that landed, probably the top of the Gill. The road's closed. If it's at our spot we know our first friend will have been found if they've anything about them. I have to admit I'm a little disappointed. There'll be an appeal on the news section of their website soon. They'll be looking for and requesting information. We'll see what they know."

He took the water bottle from the side of the cage. "You need clean water my little friend and I need to get things back to normal next week, relax more. I wonder when the urge for the challenge will begin again? I have, however, an appointment. The wait is over, our new car has arrived. How long have we waited? Do I care where the wiring loom is made? No! However, the timing couldn't have been better. We will turn from evil black to princess white – well not exactly, Lord Byron, it's silver but then beggars can't always be choosers."

***

Cyril checked the wording of the statements. The Media Manager sat like a child waiting for his work to be assessed. Cyril flicked open the file and read the first statement. It was the general appeal for witnesses. It followed a set pro-forma and was straightforward. In some ways, considering the time between the girl going missing and finding the body, he felt it was a stab in the dark but he had experienced positive results in previous difficult cases when people's memories had been jogged. His request for aerial images of Kex Gill linked to a map of the area had been acted upon and they were certainly clear. "These are good." He looked across the desk. "Many drivers know their A to B and locations but not necessarily the route between the two points. They're too busy just following their satnavs. If they drive it regularly, they take little notice."

The statement giving details that a body had now been found but no formal identification had been made at this stage, had been carefully worded and was more to reassure the police had been proactive. It clearly stated further information would be released once identification had been made and the next of kin notified. Finally, he flicked over to the last page and read the appeal for information regarding the cylinder. Photographs of the type of drainage twinwall pipe had been added to the text requesting information about similar items found, lost or stolen in the last six months. He was in possession of details confirming the name of the probable manufacturer. It was also stated that the police would handle any contact with the utmost confidence and sensitivity, intimating there could be an armistice between thief and the police.

"In other words, we'll turn a blind eye if you've nicked it," Cyril mumbled as he handed them back. "Thanks. I need to organise a face to camera appeal as soon as we have confirmation of identity. I can link everything then. We may have forty-eight hours."

Chapter 29

Dr Julie Pritchett and Dr Isaac Caner, both forensic pathologists stared at the black cylinder positioned on the stainless steel downdraft table. They understood the challenge that was before them. Julie had seen the photographs stored on the CSI supervisor's laptop showing the container in the original setting. They had all discussed the steps they were going to take and assurances had been agreed that they would not overlook anything.

Flat based wooden chocks, specifically made to suit the circumference of the tube, were positioned in three places along the table's length to give stability whilst work to remove the body was carried out. Two dedicated CSI personnel, one the supervisor on the case, were also present and they would assist in the extraction and collection of evidence during the initial part of the investigation before the autopsy was carried out. Two regular technicians were also present. Owen had never seen so many people as he watched using the large flat screen positioned directly ahead of him.

The remaining end cap had been removed and set aside for finger print and glue analysis whilst a further endoscope investigation had been carried out. It was clear from the evidence seen that the girl had certainly died whilst within the container. Severe damage to her fingernails and the resultant markings to the inner plastic wall indicated what might have been her final, desperate attempt to escape. There was also clear evidence that the shoulder area had been adhered in places to the smooth inner surface; some skin tears were visible. After collecting a small sample from the area, it was discovered that a strong-bond glue had been applied. The results from the sample would be assessed against a database of adhesives in the hope a manufacturer could be identified and an onward trail investigated.

The cylinder position was adjusted to ensure the victim faced uppermost. There appeared to be no adhesion between the upper body and the inner surface to that side. Using a fine Mopec 5000 circular autopsy saw connected to a bone dust vacuum, the cylinder was sliced down two sides; the blade normally used for cutting harder materials made short work of the corrugated plastic.

Owen watched as two CSI removed what appeared now to be a semi-circular coffin lid before it was placed on a sterile work surface. That too would go for a more detailed analysis. For the first time, the victim was revealed. Owen had seen the photographs of Sadie and he was now in no doubt, even with the arms partially cloaking her face, that it was the missing teenager. He immediately thought of her parents. Even with the marbled skin, of a greenish-blue that varied in intensity across the torso, the distended stomach area, the remains of Sadie Vance reminded him of a doll. She seemed so diminutive held within the remaining section of the confined setting, appearing to contrast starkly with the monotone plastic. There was something about her position, only dressed in her bra and pants, that immediately made him think she was ready to dive backwards and swim; she was almost fish-like in appearance, a mermaid. It was then the finality hit him. She was someone's child, she was loved and missed and now … his head spun, he felt dizzy. Instinctively, he raised himself up to stand on his toes as Julie had suggested whilst observing his first autopsy. He controlled his breathing until the light-headedness dissipated.

The technicians started photographing the body, working the three visible sides.

"Severe contusion along with a skin abrasion to the area behind and just low of the ear, limited bleeding but some clotting." Julie adjusted the strong lights attached to either side of her headband and moved closer to the area. Dropping the magnifying visor, she studied the site. She pointed and close-up photographs of the area were seen on screen as the technician moved forwards. "There appears to be some residue within the area of broken skin, probably traces left by the weapon."

Her every word and observation would be recorded throughout the process.

"There is clearly a deep section of bruising of a circular form suggesting a strike by an open-ended, tubular implement. Looking at the degree of damage, it suggests it was a forceful strike at ninety degrees to the skin." Taking a small stainless steel ruler, she laid it below the damage and more photographs were taken. "Two point five to two point seven five centimetres in diameter."

Owen immediately thought of the photographs on the Incident Room wall. The measurements had been added.

They were similar.

Julie moved quickly, identifying further damage to the wrists, ankles and the finger nails. "Signs of cadaveric spasm to the hands brought about by profuse use before death." She turned to Caner. "Lividity?"

Caner moved to look at the lower part of the body. "There appears to be fixation of post-mortem staining." He performed a blanching test by pressing the skin with his thumb. After release, the staining remained. "Lividity is fixed. She was either upright or at an angle pre and post death. She wasn't moved for a good number of hours after death. There's clearly contact flattening, no lividity to the areas in compression with the cylinder, just as we'd expect." It was all matter of fact and Julie liked it that way.

Julie nodded as she focused on the girl's face. "Asphyxiation? Evidence suggests the tube, once the covers were glued in place, would become airtight." Again, she looked at Caner who moved next to her and requested photographs of the arm position before moving them to rest on Sadie's chest, giving a clear view of her whole face for the first time – rigor mortis had ceased as the body was now in the process of putrefaction. Owing to the way the victim had been stored, airtight and hot, the black outer layer of plastic conducting the heat to the inner area, their assessment task was made far more challenging.

"Petechial haemorrhages over the face, conjunctiva. We can confirm on seeing the mucosa and pleura."

"There are clear signs of congestion and oedema over the face and viscera." She pointed to the distended stomach."

The body had not been touched other than to move the

arms and it was clear she had been murdered but there were no signs of serious abuse or maltreatment.

Julie looked at the camera and could see Owen in the top corner.

"We'll send samples for toxicology and we'll be investigating for any recent sexual activity shortly."

***

Owen had phoned an interim report through to Cyril. The Police Family Liaison Officers were already with Sadie's parents; they had worked with them from the outset and a close, professional relationship had been established. The longer Sadie had been missing, there was a developing realisation the outcome was becoming less positive. Another FLO, who had been working remotely with Jessica White's parents arranged to visit. It was important they heard first hand from them.

Cyril checked his tie and stared at himself in the mirror. He raised a finger to his eye and lowered the lid. "Bloody hell, Bennett, you could pack those bags for a fortnight." He breathed a deep sigh. In some ways he personally felt a degree of failure. He would reflect on the course of action they had taken, their hypotheses, and assumptions but in his heart of hearts, he knew there would be a second victim.

The Media Manager was waiting for him as he left the gents. A smell of coffee lingered in the corridor from the interview room and the light drone of voices talking together made his stomach flutter. He had never really overcome his nerves when dealing with large groups, particularly the press.

Cyril received the notes and entered. There was an

immediate rush for places. All went quiet. Cyril sat at the desk and adjusted the microphone. Behind was a blue backcloth featuring the North Yorkshire Police crest.

"Thank you very much for your help and support. Following the discovery of the body in Kex Gill we have now formally identified it to be that of the nineteen-year-old, Sadie Vance. Sadie has been missing for just over nine days and enquiries to establish the circumstances surrounding Sadie's death are ongoing. Sadie's family are currently being supported by our specialist liaison team and they request privacy at this difficult time.

"The police will continue to have a visible presence in the area and we're still following evidence for the safe return of the twenty-two-year-old, Jessica White."

An image of the woman appeared on the screen to his right.

"As you may be aware, a number of appeals have been made on social media but we hope this will reinforce what we need from the general public. We need them to come forward with any information, no matter how trivial they might think it is, dash cam footage or observation. Did you travel on the A59 through Kex Gill between the dates shown here? There's a map and photographs on our sites showing the area if you are unfamiliar with it. Did you see a dark coloured estate car parked nearby or in a public car park along the route within a few miles of the location?"

The photograph changed to one of the twinwall pipe. Cyril turned to look.

"Have you seen tubes, rigid drainage pipes like these? Have you had a number stolen, even one? This information is of vital importance to us. This pipe will fit in the luggage space of an estate car. Finally, have you seen deposited in the Hampsthwaite Road area, a cardboard tube similar to this?" Cyril held up the described item. "May I say again, all disclosures will be treated in the utmost confidence. The number to contact will be on screen in a moment but to go through our website will ensure we receive your comments."

Cyril picked up the glass of water and took a drink. He could feel sweat trickle down his inner arm.

"I'll take a few questions." He turned to the media officer; the questions had been submitted prior to the meeting and the officer and Cyril had selected three.

"Chris Holland, Yorkshire Post. Thank you. Can you confirm this is a murder investigation and secondly what is the significance of the pipe?"

"We're treating it as such and the pipe I cannot disclose at this point in time. However, I will say it is of crucial importance we discover more about that and more about the vehicle." He turned. "Matt?"

"Thanks, Matt Pearson, Harrogate Advertiser. Do you believe you're dealing with two kidnap victims, DCI Bennett?"

The question had been rephrased from that submitted. Cyril raised an eyebrow. "No comment, Matt."

Cyril stood. "Thank you again, no more questions. We'll keep you fully informed through the correct official channels." He looked across at the third member of the press who had submitted a question and raised an eyebrow. "Sorry, but for now, no further questions."

Chapter 30

Cyril selected a table at the front of The Little Ale House, a pub he had adopted after the closure of The Coach and Horses. His jacket was on the back of the chair. He had planned to meet Julie for a pre-dinner drink but was grateful for a moment's peace, a gap in the day where he could finalise his thoughts. His phone was positioned on the table, as if on sentry duty.

His mind was flooded with the images he had seen before leaving his office – a collage taken from the video and commentary of the initial stages of the girl's extraction. Even though it was Julie on camera, he had tried to separate his wife from the medical practitioner who worked on the young woman's body; that person to him was different, in some ways alien. Whether it be the PPE that effectively masked most of her features or the fact he emotionally needed to distance her from this work, he did not know. Those snapshots now seemed on a loop, briefly leaving his mind's eye but then returning bringing with them a degree of discomfort and sadness.

He ran a finger down the pint glass removing the droplets of condensation and revealing the clarity of the golden contents. *Will we find Jessica alive or has she already been dumped in some inhospitable place?* His thoughts tumbled more when the realisation hit that without serendipity, the accident on the moorland at that exact location, Sadie would still be in the valley and the likelihood of being discovered was as remote as the spot itself.

Julie was leaning on the short metal railing that separated the pub's yard area and the pavement and watched Cyril for a few moments. He presented a forlorn figure. Entering through the gate she rounded an empty table, leaned and kissed him on the head. The barman appeared with perfect timing.

"Could you please leave our customer in peace, doctor!" He winked. "You look as though you need a drink."

Cyril chuckled and stood.

"A large Whittaker's gin with standard tonic, please." Julie grinned. "You're rude, young man, but in this instance a life saver."

Cyril pulled out a chair. She picked up his pint and took a long sip.

"A man can have nothing!"

"Ten minutes shop talk and then nothing for the rest of the evening. Agreed?"

Cyril took back the pint and nodded.

"The autopsy results continued to show what we initially identified. Have you seen the early video report?"

Cyril nodded again.

"A single blow to the side of the head. It struck the posterior auricular, which is here." She leaned over and demonstrated on Cyril just as her drink arrived.

"That's a sensitive area." He put his hand to the point and pressed harder.

"This will cause the person to blackout as it hits some

serious nerves bringing immediate shock to the brain. He might, however, have been aiming for the temple area. Someone who knew what they were doing would choose the place they did. We found no further evidence of deliberate, inflicted injuries other than to where she was bound at the ankles and wrist. There were some lesions, skin tears where she'd broken away from the glue. Caner and I feel the gluing was done to prevent too much movement once she was in the cylinder. We're running a test using the same twinwall and a girl of Sadie's built to see if it's possible to get someone into the space or whether it would need more than one person to fulfil this gruesome task."

Cyril turned and stared at Julie. "Why have I been fixated that there was only one person involved? I must be slipping!"

"We'll have an idea by tomorrow. Where was I? Right, yes, there was a slight blade line marking the skin on her right leg but we feel that resulted accidentally when her clothes were being removed using a sharp blade. There's also evidence to suggest her underclothes were never removed. No evidence of sexual interference pre or post death is apparent, although sexual intercourse had taken place within forty-eight hours pre death. Smears taken should explain that. I've prioritised so we should get the results pretty sharpish. The sex wasn't performed under duress and it certainly wasn't rape. Common sense tells us it wasn't post death."

"According to her boss, she didn't go into work owing to period pains on the day she went missing." Cyril frowned, a degree of confusion was clearly visible on his face.

Julie slipped the lemon from the drink and bit into it. "Incorrect, a lie and an excuse."

"Another anomaly. So, the cause of death is as you first thought?"

"Asphyxiated, a slow process within the confines of the cylinder. It was very tight. We also discovered a residue of some form of lubricant, washing up liquid we think, but we await the lab results. Same with the glues used, Forensics are checking against a database of proprietary adhesives. My guess is the standard Super Glue. You'll then be able to check local suppliers regarding quantities sold to an individual or business. How was the press briefing? Caner said he caught the local television news and mumbled something about a handsome policeman."

Cyril checked his watch. "Ten minutes is up and the Italian restaurant across the road is expecting us." He finished his pint and stood, collected his jacket and slipped inside to pay. As they crossed the road, Julie mentioned there was still a chance of finding a print or DNA sample. "Manipulating someone who may have been awake and scared into the confines of that cylinder might cause a moment's carelessness. That's what we and the CSI do. We look for a killer's Achilles' heel and most times, my handsome policeman, we find it."

Cyril paused momentarily. For the first time she had mentioned the word *killer*. It may have been only one word, but it seemed to bring with it the greatest responsibility.

***

The dedicated lines set up to deal with the responses from the press releases and television appeal had brought a greater number of calls and media contacts than they had expected. Harry Nixon listened to the recording of the call made by a Fiona Grimes. He jotted down notes and the contact details before moving over to April's desk.

"There's something about this call." He handed her a piece of paper containing the details and explained. "She worked with a child in an EBD school around 2006 as a SENCO, a Special Educational Needs Coordinator. The lad exhibited a strange fixation for cardboard tubes. He would hide toy figures of different sizes in different tubes and try to steal them out of the room. She suggests there may be nothing in the action displayed but she'd seen the appeal and it was the words *no matter how trivial* made her pick up the phone. The lad would be about twenty-seven by now."

"Make arrangements, we'll see her. Where is she?"

Nixon checked the sheet. "The school was then in Bradford, Undercliffe, but it moved to a new purpose-built site in Eccleshill after that date. Grimes lives in Pool in Wharfdale." He looked up. "A bonus, close to home too!"

"Arrange a meeting. Make sure she knows it's urgent. Is she still working?"

"Now lectures part-time at the University of Leeds within teacher training."

"We'll go to her home or work whichever is the quicker."

Nixon turned to leave. "We may also need the support of the Behaviour Investigative Analyst from the sounds of it too but we can hold on that until we've the full story. The details of both missing persons have, I know, been coded into SCAS and the latest findings added."

"A Cracker, we call those analysts, how exciting." His voice was flat.

April rolled her eyes, shook her head and watched him

move to his work station. Some days she could throw something at him, something heavy. She continued to filter the many responses received. Each would be prioritised and nothing would be dismissed or discarded, no matter how bizarre the claim or the information.

***

Within four hours Harry Nixon and April drove over the bridge that crossed the River Wharf at Pool. The river was at its summer level.

"I used to fish here when I was a nipper. That bank on the left, I fished for grayling, pretty fish too. I remember my brother caught a bloody big tench on Kraft cheese slices, thought he'd hooked the river bed, no fight just weight. It's called the doctor fish for some reason. He took it home and cooked it but it tasted like bog water." He saw April turn. "Not like loo water, real bog, muddy stuff from a marsh. He thought he'd need the doctor after that! I recall that he threw up too!"

April glanced in the direction of the river. She had heard enough but said nothing. Passing the Shell petrol station, the car headed left towards Pool Bank. "It's just past the roundabout near The White Hart."

Moments later the sign for The Beeches, a collection of relatively new stone-built houses appeared on the left. Harry found the house and parked outside. The door opened before they had moved away from the roadside.

"DI Richmond?" Fiona Grimes opened the door wide. The greeting was warm. "Come through. I thought we might enjoy the garden as we chat, appreciate the good weather whilst we can unless, of course …"

"That's sounds most welcome. Yes, I'm April Richmond

and this is DC Harry Nixon. We're grateful for your cooperation. Our colleagues in West Yorkshire know we're here. We're not treading on their toes."

On entering the garden, they were greeted by another woman, a good few years older than Fiona but April immediately assumed she too was a teacher from the way she was dressed.

"Let me introduce you to an old colleague of mine, Linda Morrison. She has a doctorate but never admits to it. She was our play therapist and a wonderful one too. We worked at Willow Fold together."

"And I thought you were a teacher." April's tone suggested she was a little crestfallen.

"I was, that's how I started."

The garden seemed well-established considering the house was only a few years old. Beyond the fence was an expanse of green.

"It's the local cricket pitch. Fiona worries about her patio windows when they're playing but so far …" Linda spoke quietly, her voice naturally calming.

Fiona appeared.

"It's beautiful. May I call you Fiona?"

"Certainly, and thank you. I do love my garden. We get the afternoon sun which I adore. Before we start, please have some refreshment."

Within ten minutes they were all seated. April had set up a Dictaphone and Harry would add notes as she chatted. Their personal details were added.

"I had such a frustrating time at the school and left soon after the authority deemed the building unsuitable. It was prime for building land and had nothing to do with educational unsuitability. I went part-time teaching at the university and I also do some voluntary work in the school just up the road here. It's a vocation, like yours, you can't just stop, can you?"

Harry would have liked to challenge her wisdom but controlled his inner urge.

"I was the SENCO and I'm sure you've researched that role. You have responsibilities to the child, the parents and the school. The child comes first and you fight for what's best for them considering their individual needs and circumstances. The kids were in special education for a reason, excluded from main stream settings, often they were aggressive and unpredictable. However, considering their upbringing or should I say lack of upbringing, much of which was linked to their home circumstances, it always amazed me how well they did. They were often very loving. Some kids lived in dire family settings. Let me talk about the child I contacted you about, his name is Jamie Ryan. He came from a difficult family. His parents had split and he spent all but one day a week with his mother and three older sisters. It was believed his mother was a prostitute, probably dealing or taking drugs too. Her daughters were also not officially working, but it was felt by many that they too were on the game. The lad was often closed in his room for what could be quite extended times when the punters called."

"Was this reported?" April leaned forward.

"Certainly, but wheels moved slowly and some never moved at all. I remembered his first day. He climbed the wall bars in the hall and informed us at the top of his voice that beans make you fart. He'd probably pulled stunts like that in his mainstream school and had consequently been excluded and sent to us. He was amazed when his behaviour was ignored. As he settled and became more familiar with staff and the other children, on many occasions, he didn't want to go home. He'd climb onto the roof and wait for the taxis – all our kids were brought from and returned home by taxi, they had escorts, usually female who monitored them during the journeys. You would be amazed at what they heard. We'd a dreadful Headteacher, she was never there, too busy progressing her career. Fortunately, the Deputy was wonderful. He'd often watch the lad and when he climbed down, he or another staff member would take him home. I did my fair share but it was predominantly the Deputy."

For the first time Linda spoke. "If I may carry on with Fiona's comments on his home life. There was no evidence that he was being sexually abused nor was there evidence of any sexual activity but the doctor felt that he'd witnessed inappropriate adult sexual interaction whether that be audible or visual. From that meeting I set up the play therapy sessions to guide our thinking and it soon became clear that he had an inappropriate understanding of sex."

"I take it the child had a social worker and the school had a Police Liaison Officer?" April frowned as the picture of the boy was developing in her mind.

It was Fiona who answered with a degree of venom. "The social worker was blind, not literally you understand, maybe I should've said blinkered, frightened of her own shadow. Social workers sometimes can't do right for doing wrong like most people dealing with the general public and I'm aware of that. She'd visited both homes as the parents had separated and she'd witnessed nothing out of the ordinary – 'A clean and lovely home. The sisters love their brother.' Parents who abuse their kids emotionally are very wily. When he had visited the father, she noticed a difference in Jamie's behaviour. He seemed more open and happier but we put that down to male bonding. Christ, the social worker was barely a kid herself. I remember her words, 'They seem very nice and kind when I'm there. I have to go by what I see.'" She put a sugar lump into her tea and sat back. "It brings back the frustration just talking about the boy."

"Linda, you mentioned the play therapy."

"We kept his sessions individual after we noticed he'd withdraw if others were with him, particularly girls. With boys he would try to dominate the session and we felt we weren't witnessing the true child, if that makes sense. We wanted him to be fully engrossed in his play, believing he was unwatched and unsupervised. The room was filled with a selection of specific toys and games, all free for his use. We used a two-way mirror to observe him. In many of those observations he played with the dolls we had. We also had a junk box filled with cardboard boxes and tubes. I don't know, April, if we're making an assumption but it was this behaviour that got us to ring the dedicated police number. Fiona suggested we ring considering the girl's death and the information about the drain pipe and the cardboard tube."

April said nothing but Harry looked at her and then back at his notes.

"He would insert the dolls into them. If he'd a large tube, it would be a large doll, a small tube then maybe a plastic soldier. He'd then take one out after the session. Usually, the tube was concealed down his trousers or up his jumper. We knew but said nothing."

"What did he do with them?" April's heart rate had risen.

"He'd hide them somewhere in school, in different locations, but then on occasion, he'd take one onto the roof if he climbed that day. He'd use the tube as a spyglass when up there. He'd probably removed the figure first or he'd take another tube from the craft box. It was as if he were closing down the world to just that small circle, like he was controlling what was around him."

The word spyglass made April shiver. "What happened to Jamie?"

Chapter 31

The message on the police website brought with it excitement. Just the word Thruscross made Owen smile and a knot form in his stomach. This was the remote spot from where they had received the last phone message from Sadie's phone. After that the phone was dead. The date of that call and the intelligence now received seemed too disparate but it necessitated an immediate meeting with the person who had messaged in with the information. It took just over the hour.

Owen picked up the drone and weighed it in his hand. Barry Sutcliffe sat opposite, his arms folded.

"Was this the drone you were flying at Thruscross?"

"Yes, its light and manoeuvrable and has a great camera. 4K resolution. The next model has a zoom facility. This one's a bit flaky in strong winds but otherwise it's a good starter drone." Barry took the drone from Owen and removed the camera cover. "The camera's attached to a gimbal, that's what keeps the images really steady. It moves with the craft, but the lens remains static."

"So, Mr Sutcliffe, you were at Thruscross Reservoir when you saw the dark coloured estate? Do you remember the date?"

"Last Tuesday. It was quiet, can be mid-week but gets

very busy at weekends so I avoid those times. I arrived there later than expected. The car, you know the dark coloured estate, was in the car park that's set away from the road. It was there when I arrived. There was another car too, that one was a silvery grey."

"What did you notice about the estate?"

"Nothing, a car's a car to me. A to B, carry stuff and save your legs. I only sent a message to you folk as I heard the appeal on the radio and because it was between the dates mentioned and Thruscross is close enough to the site where the girl was found. Dreadful thing, poor lass. Did my civic duty by contacting your website. I wasn't going to ring 101, I've tried that in the past and it's a waste of bloody time. If you want my opinion but you probably don't, it's not fit for purpose."

Owen let the criticism fly over his head. It wasn't the first time he had heard it.

"Did you see the driver?" Owen expected the answer to be negative.

"When I fly, I like to stand on the picnic table, it gives me a direct view towards the dam wall, you're high up and that way I can see the drone at all times. It's a great view. That's one of the rules, keeping sight of the craft. The bloke was looking over at the slipway side, the overflow. I hadn't put the drone in the air then, just checking the wind and stuff. It was then I saw him climb onto the parapet wall and dangle his legs over the drop. To be honest, I thought we had a right nutter and he was going to jump, especially when he stood up!"

Sutcliffe paused as if replaying the moment.

"He put his arms up like this and locked them as if he

was going to dive. I couldn't take my eyes off him but then I saw him climb down and back on the road before crossing to the other side. He then stared at the water. I soon had the drone up and flew it down towards the dam. He heard it as I saw him looking for it. They're audible but not easy to see, a bit like sky larks. You can hear the little buggers but you can never see them. Any road, I knew he'd clocked it as he put his hand to his eye, a bit like a telescope. I was watching through the screen and I could see him looking directly up at me, if that makes sense."

"What happened then?"

"I brought the drone back to change the battery. I was sitting having a coffee when he approached me. I thought he was going to criticise me for disturbing the tranquillity, some folk can be a real pain. He was quite charming, asked some sensible questions. I did tell him that I didn't start to fly until he had his feet on the ground just in case he lost his balance!"

Owen said nothing hoping more information would be disclosed.

"He laughed and thanked me, can you believe. He told me he had an old friend who liked to challenge himself, stand high up and look at the world with butterflies in his stomach, that's what he said. This friend had dared him to do the same when he could, as the friend doubted that he had the courage. He tried it and found it exhilarating, seemed a strange bloody answer to me but who am I to judge. I let him look at the footage I'd taken. He was impressed."

"Do you still have it, the footage?"

"No, if I kept everything, I'd need a great deal of digital

storage. If it's not interesting I get rid … I offered to send it to him if he gave me his email but he wasn't interested."

"Did you say he held the control?"

"No, this screen." He held up the mini-iPad. "This."

"Mr Sutcliffe, I'm going to need that for evidence. It may well hold his fingerprints and from the evidence you've given so far, he may well be the man for whom we're looking."

"Shit! How long for?"

"Two days maximum. It will be assessed by our Forensic people. What's on here might just save another life." Owen had said more than he should.

"The other girl? Shit, I'm sorry now I deleted the footage. Who'd have thought. Maybe I was right thinking he was a bloody nutter."

"I'd like you to come to the station, your description of the man might be just what we need and maybe we can do the tests on the pad and you can take it when you leave."

***

"Once the children leave the security of the primary school setting, you lose them, they move on as you focus on the next tranche coming through. They then move from being the big fish in a small pond to being very small fish all over again and for some that's so traumatising. From what I know, Jamie went into a residential EBD provision. We were thinking before you came, he'll be about twenty-seven now.

"One other thing. We believe he was often locked in his room. The social worker informed us it had blackout blinds or curtains. She was told he needed total dark before he could sleep."

Linda interrupted. "He also had a trick when holding the tube to his eye. He'd cover the end with his hand and then release it as if he was making light and dark. He liked the dark. He was one of the few children who'd want the light off in the Time Out room – that was a space they were either sent to or they could go voluntarily to calm down without repercussions. It was windowless apart from a small piece of plexiglass in the door."

Fiona interrupted. "I'd forgotten that. Do you remember that he often pulled his jumper over his head too, to hide from his immediate surroundings? He liked the dark. He'd often sit in the shadows."

April paused on hearing that word again before asking for the names of the other staff who were there at the time and if they knew any at the school he went on to. The first request was easy but for the second they could not even remember the school.

"Only now are the powers that be contemplating introducing dedicated child protection agencies, but these will only succeed if they are manned by professionals who have not only the funding but the power to act without fear of litigation and ridicule. Remember, April, everyone has experienced school so they all have differing perceptions, all are experts. The answer to your question, sorry, the Local Education Authority should help."

Fiona stood.

"I do hope this hasn't been a waste of your time."

"We just need to find what happened to Jamie Ryan so we can remove him from the enquiries. We're grateful to you both, what you thought was insignificant certainly was not as your information links to what we know and this is often the key to finding the perpetrator. We may need to talk to you again if there's anything else." She handed them a card. "That's my direct mobile. Contact me anytime and I mean anytime, someone will be there to answer. One last thing. You mentioned that although the Headteacher was ineffective, the Deputy demonstrated real concern for the lad, offered a male figure. Is he still at the school?"

"Christian? He lived up to his name in all senses of the word. He cared for them all. He committed hours to the place. Where he is? I'm not sure. It would only take you a phone call to find out."

Within minutes of leaving the house April had set the wheels in motion. The details had been sent and she hoped before arriving back in Harrogate she would have some answers. She felt an inner buzz of excitement.

Chapter 32

Cyril had felt the same buzz on hearing the information from Owen and the detailed report sent by Harry Nixon. Maybe technology had its positive side.

The results came through from pathology. The semen DNA from the smear test matched that of Sadie's boyfriend. He had given the sample at interview and it matched. Toxicology showed she had consumed alcohol, marijuana, the girl would not have been in a position to drive and may have been temporarily incapacitated. There was nothing in the details they had not considered. The notes were added to the Incident Room board.

Cyril read the notes. According to the records held by the Bradford LEA, Jamie Ryan had attended Wingate residential EBD school after leaving Willow Fold. He remained, if that's the correct term, until the summer of 2010. He was at that stage still living with his mother during the school holidays. There was evidence that he was reluctant to go home and the school roof proved to be a continued sanctuary when they closed for holidays or when he simply left a room and walked out. It was as if he could climb glass. The psychologist's reports showed a deterioration in his overall behaviour at school. It was recorded that he would refuse to sleep in his bed, he slept under it. There were a number of reports of violence towards the younger pupils and he was often isolated from the group as a punishment. There was no further opportunity for exclusion. On one occasion, when on the roof, he started to remove the slates and throw them at his peers. In contrast, however, recorded interviews with his mother suggest he was fine at home and still enjoyed the solitude of his room. He was never any bother, he loved his sisters and would do what they asked. There was no record of his attending school after a certain date. Neither they, nor his parents heard from him again.

Cyril turned to Smirthwaite. "Missing on July 13th 2010."

Brian moved to a computer. "A Tuesday, schools usually finish on a Friday."

"He is still on the police missing persons' register."

April entered the room. "Wingate School was an old stone manor house set in its own grounds. According to the records the school tried to balance academic achievement with outdoor activities, assault courses, sailing, that sort of thing, alongside more vocational challenges. The philosophy promoted was the kids had failed in a normal school environment so an alternative approach to learning was devised."

"And?" Brian asked. "Sounds like a good idea to me. We're not all academics."

"It failed its first Ofsted inspection and a new Head was brought in. This was before Jamie arrived. After the second inspection it was classed as 'outstanding'. That's some jump. The Headteacher was hailed as a genius." April paused as she looked at them both. "It failed the third inspection, went into special measures, that means it went back to where it was in the first place. Zero to Hero and back to zero. The place closed in 2012 and now it's a housing estate. The head left, took early retirement after a breakdown."

"He was shoved I bet. Had Jamie anything to do with the place's demise?"

April shrugged her shoulders. "Again, according to LEA records, the Deputy at Willow Fold, the primary school, who, according to Fiona Grimes, had taken a liking to Jamie, was a Mr Christian Fletcher."

On hearing the name Cyril immediately thought of *HMS Bounty* but then realised that was a Fletcher Christian. "Sorry, distracted!"

April smiled understanding the confusion. "He stayed at Willow Fold until 2009."

"What do we know about him?"

"He's single. Took early retirement. It's believed there was a bereavement within the family and he inherited his parents' estate. I spoke with a member of staff at the school and they suggested he'd become disillusioned. He'd inherited quite a lot of money and saw no further need to work. His words were, 'psychologically broken'."

"I'd do the same," there was sincerity in Brian's voice.

"Where is he now?"

According to the Voters' register and his driver's licence he lives in Peter Lane, Burton Leonard."

Cyril looked at April and then Brian. "Lovely, close to us but a long way from Bradford. Get Owen to accompany you and pay him a visit. See if he can shed any light on this Jamie Ryan character. What's your gut saying, April?"

April smiled. She turned to the whiteboard and let her finger rest on the word, penumbra. "Jamie's got to still be alive. So far, we have nothing other than a missing person report and that continues to add to the characteristics and foibles we've seen throughout this case. It does tell me, however, that our eyes might just be growing accustomed to the dark and we might soon be in a position to look more deeply into the shadowlands."

***

The police operator recorded the call that came in with information about a dark coloured estate car.

"Pateley Bridge south car park, the one down by the cricket pitch. It was there. Dark blue hybrid Skoda estate. I've wanted one for a while so I waited to talk to the owner who turned out to be a right ignorant sod, bloody rude too." The voice on the telephone seemed excessively loud.

"When was this, sir?"

"Tuesday, afternoon. I was checking the tickets in the car park here at Pateley Bridge, the one over the bridge by the children's play area. He had something long that stretched through the car to the passenger seat back. I couldn't see what it was exactly as it was covered with a blanket. There were some bags of cement in there too. Impressive carrying capacity them Skoda estates."

"Would you recognise him if you saw him again?"

"Tried to forget the miserable sod. Remember he had a beard, he was well-groomed. Wore sunglasses, it was a good day. Bright. Anyway, just thought I'd call as you're looking for a dark estate and a pipe. The object stashed in the back could've been just that."

The operator took his details and thanked him but it

seemed a long shot.

***

April had checked Google Earth to see that Peter Lane was narrow. Cottages lined one side. Realising there was limited space for vehicles she parked on the main road.

Owen checked the house details and pointed to a stone cottage about half way down the lane. A silver Volkswagen was parked to the front of the garage. Owen went and put his hand on the bonnet, it was cold. He noticed the person in the back garden by the wooden shed.

"Mr Fletcher!" Owen shouted louder than he had planned and he noticed the man drop the trowel he was holding. "Sorry, didn't mean to startle you."

Fletcher frowned and picked up the tool. "May I help you?"

"Are you Christian Fletcher?"

"I am. And you are?" He then noticed April appear.

"DI David Owen and this is DI Richmond. You'll have guessed, the police." Owen held out his ID.

"Yes, I'm Christian Fletcher. How may I help you?"

"We just need a few minutes of your time."

"We're trying to locate a child you taught, Jamie Ryan." Both officers could see Fletcher's shoulders sink.

"Our Jamie, that's a chapter in my life I'll never forget and some of my life I shall not get back. One of the hardest years I experienced in any school. He was a very disturbed boy and it didn't help when we had an inept system of monitoring through Social Services, compounded by the Headteacher's ineptitude. It was a year I was determined to put behind me. I tried to keep track of Jamie for a while after his leaving. He went on to Wingate Residential if my memory serves me well. Like us, I don't think they had success with him and I believe the school had some mixed fortunes with dear old Ofsted."

"Was he a violent child?"

"I remember him arriving, he came to us late in his primary school career, he was in year six, probably later than he should, but that's credit to the mainstream school trying to keep him with them. My experience suggests that's not always what's best for the child. But asked if he were violent? No, not to the others but he had some strange ways when playing with toys – soldiers, dolls and Action Man type figures. He hid them in toilet tubes and the like. Once he'd settled with us, he had long spells where he didn't want to go home so he'd climb on to the roof."

"If you knew it was going to happen, didn't you try to stop him?"

Fletcher laughed and seemed to relax for the first time since their arrival. "Have you tried stopping an eleven-year-old who can get where dirt can't and climb glass to boot? Yes, but if he was determined … we were trained in restraint but I never liked taking that approach as some could get violent and … but that's not important. I'd watch him to make sure he didn't do anything stupid when he was aloft. Once his taxi had gone, he'd come down. I or a free member of staff would take him home."

April was the next to speak. "I interviewed Fiona Grimes who explained the difficulties the child faced. She also expressed her admiration for your dedication not only to the school but also to Jamie."

"That's nice, I'll have it carved on my headstone when they bury me with a stick of chalk. Dedication can be a shallow master as I'm sure you're only too aware. Fiona was a professional and a very clever girl, perceptive. When I had a bad day, too many plates spinning, she used to say 'never let the doubters win.' Dr Linda Morrison was good for the school too, saw through the crap. She was the one who first spotted his unusual behaviour with the figures. I did my best for each child in our care. I suppose I had a soft spot for Jamie. I had an unusual upbringing myself and I suppose you can draw a parallel. Maybe I saw him as a shadow of me. I suppose you could say I was a poacher who became a gamekeeper, but alas, it's all behind me thank goodness. I retired here to this wonderful spot and before you ask, my father brought me to this village when I was eleven; to a caravan in a field over yonder during my holidays." He pointed over his shoulder in an approximate direction. "It was nothing exotic but I loved the freedom and being away from my mother but that's another story. When I finished teaching, I retired early, I was lucky enough to be left some money. This place seemed a natural location to spend retirement. I wanted a bungalow but I fell in love with this cottage."

"Have you heard about the missing Harrogate girl? Her body's now been found. Fiona saw the connection between Jamie's behaviour and the circumstances of the girl's death." She handed him her electronic tablet showing the photograph of the girl and the plastic twinwall pipe. "You're an intelligent man, Mr Fletcher, you can put two and two together. Does it stir memories of Jamie Ryan to you? It did for both Fiona and Linda."

Fletcher handed back the tablet and nodded his head. "Are you saying …" he did not finish the sentence but put his hand to his mouth. "How dreadful! Yes, I see what they mean."

On leaving, April slipped the electronic pad into a forensic bag and winked at Owen. "Just checking if Mr Fletcher is known to us."

***

Barry Sutcliffe sat with the e-fit specialist and answered the questions as best his nerves would allow. This was his first visit to the inside of a police station and he felt decidedly uncomfortable, and in many ways, he regretted making contact. Eight faces were now on screen.

"Look at each carefully and chose the one that best resembles the man."

Barry stabbed a finger at one. "The sunglasses were slightly larger and the beard was greyer, shorter, stubble. He didn't have the glasses when he was down by the dam only when he approached."

He was then presented with a number of questions and slowly the face on the screen changed as his comments were interpreted.

"I saw him and yet I didn't. Bloody hell, if I'd have kept the drone footage there'd be no need for all this palaver. I saw his hands on my screen more than his face. He had his hand to his eye when he was staring at the drone, as I said no sunglasses then."

With more questioning and adjustments eight more faces filled the screen.

"That's him, bloody hell, that's clever!" Barry lifted his glasses before leaning towards the screen again. "Bob on that." A huge grin spread across his face.

When he left the station, he was a happy man. His iPad

had been returned. He climbed into the car that was arranged to take him home.

The e-fit was being made ready to be circulated within the police internal system. It was compromised by the sunglasses. As Owen's car approached Harrogate, he checked his phone. The e-fit image was already there. "The chap seen with a black estate near Thruscross." He laughed. "To be honest it could be anybody. If you wanted a comedic disguise, you've got yourself a perfect example, just needs a hat! It's too old for Jamie Ryan if you ask me." He held it for April to catch a glimpse and then turned it back. "They'll have us believe in fairies some members of the public."

Chapter 33

The morning briefing was busier than expected. A great deal of intelligence had been collected and collated, some of which had already been acted upon. The e-fit filled the full flat screen at the far end of the room and had been the butt of a number of derogatory remarks. Owen had received a message informing him that the prints found on the drone pilot's iPad did not match those in the IDENT1 database. It came as a disappointment.

Cyril opened the meeting but spoke only briefly. "We've received a great deal of intel from the appeals and the team is working through it. You know the system and we must be patient. Our priority must be to find Jamie Ryan."

Owen responded, "If we couldn't find the two missing girls, how do we find someone who's been missing for years? The lad wasn't stable, he seemed to enjoy being in high places. My guess is he went permanently missing deliberately to lose a life he hated, permanently dark if you get my meaning. We could be searching for someone who is no longer alive."

Shakti recalled Harry's conversation about the Humber Bridge. "The Humber Bridge? I believe it's responsible for the disappearance of many. Owen may have a point."

"Sir." The Behaviour Investigative Analyst who was standing by one of the white boards spoke and moved forward.

"Bloody hell it's the Cracker! In for some weird hypothesis now." Nixon winked at April.

"This e-fit was created by the witness who saw someone sitting and then standing on the dam wall facing the overflow outlet at Thruscross Reservoir. That's high and the parapet is quite narrow. He suggests he used his hand to look at the drone, a bit like a telescope, both recognisable traits of Jamie Ryan. He also had a dark coloured estate. We have a witness who's yet to be fully questioned who saw a dark blue estate in a car park in Pateley Bridge on the same day. We haven't interviewed the witness but according to the recording of the conversation he had with control he described him as wearing sunglasses and he had a beard." A finger pointed to the screen. "That's two individuals who possibly saw the same man. He reported the boot area of the car as containing a long object and a number of bags of cement. The object was covered with a blanket."

Owen concentrated realising he might have been hasty.

The Analyst continued. "The described behaviour of this person shows clear signs of unease and anxiety. He demonstrated a curiosity regarding what the drone had seen, so much so, he approached the pilot asking relevant and intelligent leading questions. Why? And after seeing the footage he refused the offer to have it sent to an email account. Why? Now our second witness tried to have a conversation about the car but the owner wasn't interested. Why does our driver converse with one but try to avoid the other? The driver said he had to drop someone off but he was alone in the car. Drop someone off. Maybe he wasn't lying. In the rear luggage area was something long next to bags of cement. This was the same day remember as he was seen at the reservoir. We'll be interviewing the car park attendant more fully later today and we'll be showing the e-fit."

April looked at Owen. "If it's our killer, he hasn't put the cylinder in the reservoir at this point has he? Bags of cement – concrete boots? First, he made a visit to check the ground, and let's not forget he may have done that previously when it was the location of the last call from Sadie's phone. Did he get the idea then? If he were comfortable, he'd go back at night and …"

Owen put his head in his hands and rubbed his forehead. "Would a body in a pipe surrounded by a shed full of space float? In my opinion, even with bags of cement it wouldn't sink. He couldn't test the theory. Once it was in the reservoir, he wasn't going to get it out in a hurry, not in the dark."

"Relative densities. Density, mass and volume." Cyril's voice seemed calm. "Owen is right. You'd have to be sure. I don't think it's there and I don't think we should waste resources looking."

***

The car park attendant stood in the reception area. Smirthwaite went to meet him. After discussing the meeting held with the suspect, Brian pushed the e-fit across the table. There was an immediate response.

"That's the chap. Would have loved to see him without the shades. Ignorant git."

"Thanks very much. We may need you to look at a few real people and see if you can pick him out at some time in the future."

"Happily."

***

April's phone vibrated and shimmied across the desk. Frustrated, she answered it and her mood changed immediately. "Yes!" she screeched before calling for Owen.

Owen appeared in a hurry carrying his mug of tea, the steady stream of overflowing liquid ran down his left trouser leg but he was oblivious. "Lottery win?"

"We have a match. The prints taken from the tablet I gave to Fletcher match with ones found on the pad owned by the drone pilot. Our man was one and the same."

"Fletcher didn't have a beard," Owen mumbled, his voice flat.

"Possibly has a razor!"

Owen nodded and more liquid was spilled. "His car's silver."

"Check with DVLA if our Mr Fletcher has changed his car in the last week. If he has, we require a warrant, we need to plan a visit and that visit must be thorough."

Chapter 34

Owen summarised the updated findings.

"He traded in a dark blue Skoda estate the day after he'd been seen at Thruscross and Pateley Bridge. Now registered in his name is a silver Volkswagen, the car we saw. We have also located the Skoda estate and fortunately it's still waiting to be prepared for sale. It will be in the hands of Forensics shortly."

Cyril smiled. "Funny how that chance word, *penumbra*, has haunted this case from nearly the outset. If Fletcher is our man, he's been true to that word; he's been a shadow hiding within the shadow and laying trails using his victims' known foibles. He'd observed them and he's used them. The question is …" He looked at both April and Owen in turn. "Why? Why did he hope that Ryan might be the scapegoat or has Ryan disappeared permanently at the hands of Fletcher, and if so, what did he want to cover up?"

"We'll be paying Mr Fletcher a visit at dawn tomorrow and according to this phone's weather app, that will be 04.55. We have cars already situated locally monitoring the exit routes from the village. One armed unit, SENCO, cadaver and drug dogs are on standby. He'll be brought here. Everything must be executed to the letter. We're dealing with a clever and scheming individual." Owen watched as Cyril nodded his approval.

***

Fletcher sat in the garden of the cottage. The wooden shed door was open. On the table before him was the cage.

"You like the sunshine don't you, Lord Byron. I'm not too keen. Not good for you too much sun. Bad for the skin. I can hear Jamie now. His words still ring in my ears. He wanted to try the pipe and laughed when he squeezed himself inside. I helped of course. We'd chatted a lot on those journeys home when he was a confused child. He trusted me you see, we shared our grief in a way. He told me what went on in the house. It wasn't all innocence and light, quite the opposite. His sisters were cruel to him. Young women can be so controlling, scheming and selfish. They'll tell you it's their hormones but my mother was just the same. It was then I realised he had no future.

"I really hadn't expected what came a few years later. It was a letter, I know it off by heart: 'My dear teacher. Today was the best and the worst day of my life! I'm sure you remember very well the three o'clock boy perched aloft but far from aloof. You looked up as I down. I was the boy, alone and rejected, rejected, that is, apart from you and some of your caring colleagues. Where has the time gone? Only now, when my world seems more in focus, do I remember how much they all fought for me, a fight against the odds – ignoring my anger and impossible ways you could see through the shadows. I just wanted to tell you, sir, I was listening! How we change as we grow! I'm sorry and hope you can forgive me'.

"I knew he'd turn up and a few days later he appeared.

He'd had enough, needed help like I always did. He was homeless! What could I do? It was only after I had welcomed him in did I hear the truth."

The hamster shuffled in the soil at the base of the cage.

"He reminded me of that bitch of a Headteacher, Dorothy. She made promises to me. 'Christian if you help me, you'll go far, you'll be a Headteacher yourself very soon. Nearly everybody was disingenuous but she was the worst, she was a farmer of false hope. She neither cared for the children nor her staff, she only cared for herself."

The hamster climbed into the wheel and the steady thrum brought a certain calm.

"Do you remember *The Highwayman*, that wonderful poem?" He ran his fingers slowly across the cage bars and the hamster darted into the safety of the willow tube. "It's about love, courage and sacrifice, about keeping a promise. I made a promise. I promised to be there if Jamie ever needed help. I told him that all the staff loved him, I remember telling him that I loved him and cared for him, that's why he wanted me to drive him home. I truly cared and I said it to many of the children to calm their troubled minds. That's all they needed, to know someone was there for them. They would never come to collect, they knew that it was just words, reassurance they craved at a certain time in their troubled lives, a stepping stone to help them cross a difficult stream on their journey through life. That was until Jamie came – riding, riding a stolen bike! I remember the day as if it were yesterday. I even remember his words. 'You promised to be there for me if ever I needed help. I need help, please'.

"It was a short time after that he told me about the girl. I knew it was the truth, it was in his eyes, truth had blended with his tears forming a heady cocktail of utter fear and confusion. He still carried with him the cardboard tube with which he'd struck her. He showed it to me, demonstrated, boasted and yet he was terrified. He wasn't a kid any more, he was an adult. He'd struck her with it, she'd laughed at him, he said. She'd promised to … but then she'd laughed. After the blow, he told me he'd wrapped her face with cling film, it was close to hand. I then couldn't trust him, Lord Byron, he could do the same to me. It was when I thought about things as I looked at the night sky that I put the pieces together and I knew one thing would then lead to another. He had shone the light into the darkest recess of my mind and kindled a feeling that possibly had been dormant since childhood. I had no option but to ensure he would not return."

Christian stood, moved to the garage and removed the ladders.

"Unlike Jamie, I don't climb glass." He leaned them against the guttering before sitting again. "When Jamie was a child, he would often stare through the tube, stare at me from on high, aloof and aloft. He knew I watched out for him. It was then that he knew he had some kind of control of his life and in a strange way, I admired him. I, on the other hand, was not in control of mine, I never had been if I were honest with myself. I was beaten long ago, kept in the dark by bullying and manipulative parents and I gave in, I complied, and showed no courage, no fight whatsoever. What was the reward for my cowardice, my lack of integrity and backbone, I hear you ask? It was an education and a job and then ultimately this!" He ran an extended arm in an

254

arc as if showing off the house. "I had money in my bank from the old bastards' estate and this wonderful home, but more importantly, it enabled me to escape prematurely from the work that controlled me. You will despise me, Lord Byron, as I despise myself. I also know they know – the police that is – the electronic tablet she handed me was such a crude and deliberate ploy. But now is the time, time to show the courage I know I have, it's time for sacrifice. Soon those beastly Assyrians will come down from the fold and we will keep any future friends from harm."

He stood and filled the kettle. The hamster was silent.

"'What about me?' I hear you ask, Lord Byron. I have catered for you."

Christian picked up the cage and opened the side gate. Turning right he walked down Peter Lane, crossed the road and the green before entering the grounds of the village primary school. Security now was everywhere, even here. Eventually the door to the school clicked and opened.

"Mr Fletcher, is that Lord Byron?" The school receptionist welcomed him warmly.

"It is. As I've said, I'll be away for a while and I'm thrilled your lovely children will give my little friend here a good home. Thank you."

Fletcher turned to leave. He had a statement to write. There would be no more hiding, no more darkness, no more friends.

"Have a good holiday. He'll be loved and cared for here with us until you return."

The words made him shiver.

Chapter 35

It was late evening, Christian Fletcher had deliberately left the front and back doors unlocked. The envelope containing his statement and the handwritten note he had received from Jamie was marked with the words, *'Never let the doubters win'*. It was written in neat black copperplate script; a fine red line had been neatly struck through as if corrected by a teacher's hand. It sat on the kitchen table weighted down by a small monocular.

He checked the time. It was 02.55. The summer night was warm, the sky clear. Collecting a bottle of brandy and a thick travel blanket, the same one that had concealed the pipes, he popped them in a rucksack before climbing the ladder. Once on the tiles he scrambled towards the chimney. With one foot on either side of the ridge, he positioned the folded blanket along the crest of the tiles and sat resting his back against the stone stack; what was left of the blanket he used to wrap around his legs. He took a swig of brandy, it initially caught in his throat making him splutter but it brought to him an immediate warmth. He stared at the stars and then the slice of moon that seemed to rip the black curtain sky. The Alfred Noyes' poem came again to mind. "'Death at every window; And hell at one dark window.'"

He stared at the moon. "The hours will now crawl by like years." He pulled the cork from the bottle again and took another drink.

Chapter 36

Christian saw the lights of approaching vehicles. The mono-coloured palette of the night sky was soon broadening and blending with the eastern dawn bringing with it a freshness to a new day. They came like bees to a hive from all directions, silent and ordered. He tried to count them but soon gave up. He suddenly realised how pointless it was. Some of the vehicles parked close to the house and were now partially hidden by the roof's guttering. He heard the voices, sharp and ordered and the doors open. Figures appeared in the still semi-dark of the garden. He was now Jamie, the boy on the roof. The dawn had brought with it a milk wash of soft light. The cars, now more visible reminded him of the school taxis. Faces looked up but Christian's attention was focused on a big man standing by his car, it was the man who had called yesterday – DI Owen.

Curling his hand, Christian brought it to his eye and stared at the officer. "I see you DI Owen. I watch you and you watch me. I knew, nearer and nearer you came, your face is like a light."

Owen nodded and looked at the ladder. The two armed officers standing on the fringe of the garden had a clear view of the target. Owen quickly realised there was no real threat and held up a hand. The weapons were lowered but were still ready if needed as he watched Christian Fletcher stand, scramble clumsily onto the chimney and spread his arms. The brandy bottle he still held in his right hand before throwing both hands above his head like a diver.

Owen immediately thought the worst, "Oh, shit, he's going to bloody jump!"

"It's time, Inspector Owen, it's time. I killed them all, all three, including Jamie. I'm not really sorry, just sorry it's over. We all make sacrifices. We all have to face the truth. I let my doubters win, you see, but then you know that, that's why you're here." The voice from above seemed hollow, but so sincere and tinged with a degree of regret.

Cyril moved into the house and the smell of fried bacon filled his nostrils. He immediately saw the items on the table. Picking up the envelope he extracted the sheets of paper before moving to the window. He read the opening part of the statement. "Bloody hell!" There was anger in his voice as he slipped it back into the envelope, put it back on the table before moving outside.

Owen watched Christian lower himself, sit on the chimney edge before returning to the ridge. He stood the brandy bottle on the level and moved towards the ladder. Within minutes he was down. Officers walked forward but Owen held his hand out for a second time and they halted. Christian saw Owen's action.

"Thank you. I'm finished. It's time. I didn't have the courage to do what I had planned to do. When you're standing on the edge ... I wasn't as brave as Bess was in The Highwayman poem. Where shall I go now?"

Owen frowned as the name Bess brought immediate confusion. He pointed to an officer who moved forward holding handcuffs. Christian obliged by offering his wrists. Within minutes he was in a car and the SOCO team moved into the house, garage and shed. In time, the dogs would be used.

Chapter 37

"DNA of Sadie Vance and Jessica White was found in the boot of the estate car." April folded her arms. There was frustration and anger in her voice. "You read the statement. He was weak. I doubt we'll ever know what truly went on between teacher and pupil on those journey's home."

***

Cyril watched the interview on screen.

"Jamie confessed to me, Inspector Owen, told me it was uncontrollable anger and he didn't mean to kill the girl. He didn't know what to do. He was homeless and broke. He remembered I said I'd help. He found me, came on a stolen bicycle. I suppose we were too alike, we both had baggage. He never told me where he'd hidden the woman he'd killed but I was assured she'd never be found. I now believe that to be wrong. Tell me she was."

Owen nodded. "Go on."

"I'd told him about Dorothy, how certain women manipulated to get what they wanted, like his mother and sisters, he said. I suppose it was he who sowed the seed, said he doubted I could have done it to Dorothy. Hell, he was wrong. I hated the bitch. I've always been a coward, you see. It was when he said he could do it again, it was a fear at first but then came the fire, the excitement that he instilled in me."

"You killed him? You were afraid this doubter would win."

"He opened my eyes, made me see. It was as if I had moved from the dark into the light. I could see it could be achieved."

"The road to Damascus." Owen let the words slip from his lips.

"Indeed, Inspector, we all have Damascene moments in our lives. You have my statement. You know where he is and the woman too. I have no regrets."

Owen looked at April and at the solicitor.

"I couldn't let the doubters win." A smile came to his lips as a contradictory tear ran down his cheek before he mumbled the verse of a poem:

"To-day I shall be strong,
No more shall yield to wrong,
Shall squander life no more;
Days lost, I know not how,
I shall retrieve them now;
Now I shall keep the vow
I never kept before.

Don't let the doubters win, don't let them win ..."

No one said a word. The silence palpable. Owen had heard enough. He stared at his hands; his fingers deliberately splayed on the table top before joining them to form fists. He despised the man sitting opposite, a man who had taken the light and the life from innocent women for what seemed to him to be some strange vendetta, a vicarious reason that seemed shrouded in his disturbed thinking. Any tolerance he might have had vanished, replaced by a deep resentment. Turning to look at April he could read her facial expression.

She immediately read the situation and observed the tension build within her colleague. She quickly stood. "There's nothing more to be done here, DI Owen." The only sympathy she had was for the solicitor, whose façade seemed to crumble when more details were revealed. He now seemed isolated trying to sort some sense and order out of what they had witnessed. The solicitor watched her stand and she knew that he felt the same sense of revulsion.

"How does one defend the indefensible?" The solicitor's whispered words drifted across the table like a departing spirit.

Owen stood and left the Interview Room. He let his fist strike the wall. He had endured enough of this day. The callous depravity of the mentally troubled made his anger bubble within. They were pointless killings that brought nothing but pain to families. Seeing Owen leave the room, Cyril turned from the screen and intercepted him in the corridor. He was resting his forehead against the wall, his arms now to his side. He could read his colleague and friend's tortured expression better than any book.

"He's an exception, Owen, He's organised and deranged, and as we know that's an unpredictable combination. I know it's hard right now to find a perspective in all of this but I want you to remember there's still a great deal of good in this world, you prove that every day. We're just the ones always handling the shitty end of life's stick.

Our work will not bring back the dead but it will take someone evil off the streets and that's a positive, it's a job well done. We can never predict how personal circumstances will affect the individual, turn good to evil, but I can only hope we will make our part of the world a better and safer place for those we love and cherish. Now go home, you've done all you can." He placed a hand on his shoulder.

Cyril had read Owen's mood perfectly. He knew he needed healing and he knew that would be done when he wrapped his arms around his son. He would then understand his true value and identify his real purpose in life.

Featured Artist

It gives me a great deal of pleasure when readers not only make positive comments about this series, but also about this feature I include in each book. Art is a passion of mine, a passion I transferred to Cyril Bennett and I love including art and artists within these tales. Wherever possible, I highlight those born in Yorkshire or works I own or have had the pleasure to own. Sadly, this artist is still on my wish list.

John Atkinson Grimshaw
1836 – 1893
Gaslights, Wet streets and Moon shadows.

Atkinson Grimshaw was born in Leeds, a Victorian-era artist best known for his nocturnal scenes and urban landscapes. He is revered today as one of the most creative nightscape painters who was clearly a master of colour, lighting and shadow. Looking into many of his paintings you are walking hand in hand whilst smothered in nocturnal light, whether that be gaslight or the light of the moon. You can see why my character, Christian, was fascinated by his work and the poem.

The artist's love of realism stemmed from his passion

for photography. A self-taught artist he used the camera obscura or lenses to project images onto the canvas overcoming his insecurity as a draughtsmanship and use of perspective.

James MacNeill Whistler said of Atkinson Grimshaw's work, 'I considered myself the inventor of nocturnes until I saw Grimmy's moonlit pictures.'

The Harrogate Mercer Art Gallery has two paintings by this artist in the collection. They are: *In the Gloaming or A Yorkshire Home.* I prefer the first title and you will see why if you investigate. The second and my favourite is entitled, *Silver Moonlight.*

Leeds Art Gallery has a growing collection of one of their finest sons.

Acknowledgements

It is hard to believe we are on book twelve, so much water has passed through the valleys of North Yorkshire since the first book, *Only the Dead*. The characters have moved on, their lives intertwined in many ways as they faced both the highs and lows within their professional and personal lives.

Authors often say that the writing is a lonely pastime but I feel blessed to be surrounded by so many of these characters who seem to whisper to me as I write – they are real, they live and breathe in my imagination and like me, they grow wiser and older. I am also blessed with having a great deal of support to help the reader step into the pages. I would like to say a huge thanks to them for bringing *The Damascene Moment* to publication:

Debbie has been a wonderful support and a voice of reason throughout my writing career. Thank you, it would not have been possible without you.

To Helen Gray who has kindly checked each and every word, offered her guidance and encouragement, again I offer a massive thanks.

My thanks to Andy Barrett for his guidance with the SENCO scenes, to How Stean Gorge for their support, The Harrogate Tea Room, it has become a regular setting for Cyril and the team. When using real places within these books I like to seek permission. The manager of the Crown Hotel was most helpful to allow me free access to get a feel for the building and the setting. I would also thank the Team Rector, Simon Dowson of St John's Church for his kind support. The Mercer Art Gallery is always worth a visit.

There is also the necessity to credit the literary work I have used within the story: It was my pleasure to feature a small part of one of my favourite poems by Alfred Noyes – *The Highwayman*.

The Shadowlands, based on the life of C. S. Lewis.

I took a verse from 'How Clear, How Lovely Bright', by A. E. Housman. Written in 1880 it seemed to fit so perfectly the confused mind of the killer. Interestingly, Colin Dexter used the final line of the poem to inspire the ultimate Inspector Morse novel, Housman being Morse's favourite poet – *A Remorseful Day*. However, that too was borrowed from Shakespeare!

There are many book bloggers and readers who, through their enthusiasm and dedication put the wind beneath my wings. I cannot name them all here but I shall name a few, Sarah Hardy, Lynda Checkley, Dee Groocock, Craig Gillan, Donna Morfett, Donna Wilbor, Caroline Vincent (my guardian angel), Ian and Gill Cleverdon, Jennifer Sutherland. My thanks is extended widely.

Thanks too to the many book clubs, especially UKCBC and Sam for your support this year. To Susan Hunter, Susan Hampson and Richard Graham Judd, to Andrew Forsyth and Geoff Blakesley for your fantastic encouragement and support over the series.

Thanks to Mike at The Hub, St Thomas's Church, Up Holland. It's good to see my books there.

As you can imagine, I could go on. Authors do not write alone!

Finally, to close, it is to you, the person holding the paperback or the Kindle, the reader to whom I send my heartfelt thanks. Without you there would be little point in my writing the series. It is gratifying to see readers, not only from the UK, but from across the world are now discovering DCI Cyril Bennett. I receive many wonderful messages that fill me with the enthusiasm to write more. Thank you.

If you have enjoyed this book or the series, please tell family and friends as word of mouth is the best way to bring more people to the Harrogate Crime Series.

Until book 13!!

Malcolm

Website:

www.malcolmhollingdrakeauthor.co.uk
